He Said She Said

WHAT READERS ARE SAYING ABOUT *HE SAID, SHE SAID* ...

"We've all joked 'Was it good for you?' *He Said, She Said* gives us the answer to that question — how an individual sexual encounter was experienced and enjoyed by the other person, and what moments they found unforgettable (and worth repeating!). What a deliciously fun book! And a fitting prelude to lots of cold showers, or well ..."

"Wow. The storytelling is superb. In an era when erotic fiction sometimes makes headlines even when the characters are poorly developed, the dialogue is unlikely, and the word choices make you cringe, *He Said, She Said* is a refreshing find. The writing transports you into the most intimate of moments. I dare you to read this book and not be left quivering with arousal."

"With every story I read, it was like I was there, a voyeur to their intoxicating love affair, desperate to know what happened next … whether her take on each experience would mirror his, finding myself lost in the sensory details, the titillating plot twists, ultimately asking myself, 'Could I dare to love this unabashedly? Could my partner and I be this mutually satisfied if we spoke our truths in the bedroom, trusted deeply, and discounted every inhibition that was so engrained? What would happen if we devoted ourselves to the simple art of loving and being loved, satisfying and being satisfied? Could we have this kind of magic too?'"

"As I was reading, I kept wondering about the authors — are they lovers or just co-authors? Is this fiction, or memoir? In the end, it really doesn't matter. Because what I know to be true is that it's FANTASTIC. I will be awaiting their next book with a kind of eagerness I've never felt for a collection of stories. I read this book in one sitting and didn't want it to end."

"My wife and I read this book together. One story each night for 12 nights. Let's just say is was a pretty inspiring 12 nights at our house!"

"This is sex therapy in a book, but way more fun than you've ever imagined. Seriously."

He Said She Said

VICTOR GIBBS & MEGAN BLACK

12 UNCENSORED TALES OF LOVE AND LUST

Book #1 in the Kiss & Tell Series

Smitten books

He Said, She Said: 12 Uncensored Tales of Love and Lust

Copyright 2021 by Victor Gibbs and Megan Black

All rights reserved.

Published by Smitten Books
New York, NY
www.SmittenBooks.com

All rights reserved. No portion of this book may be reproduced, scanned, sold, or distributed in any printed or electronic form without the express written permission of the authors.

Editing, cover design, and typesetting by:
Zelda Gillian

First edition, February 2021

ISBN: 978-1-948238-49-6

Library of Congress Control Number: 2021902739

Created in the United States of America

DEDICATION

To every man and woman who dared to imagine — then went on to discover — how beautiful it could be if mind-blowing physical intimacy was matched in intensity by love, romance, respect, and trust. Because, ultimately, it's that very combination that makes the storied "once-in-a-lifetime" relationships not just possible ... but purposeful, meaningful, and transformative.

You are the lucky few among us who know that "making love" is not a euphemism, but an actual process of growing deeper in love with your partner through an adventure that is life-altering and precious.

We hope you'll use this book as inspiration to love, play, and explore ... to try something new or turn a long-held fantasy into reality. Go ahead ... love your love life!

TABLE OF CONTENTS

Chapter 1: The Most Beautiful Woman in the World 1

Time Out: A Note from the Authors 7

Chapter 2: Velcro Skirt 9

Chapter 3: Umbrella 17

Chapter 4: Finally 25

Chapter 5: Cheeky Panties 35

Chapter 6: Trust 45

Chapter 7: Dessert 53

Chapter 8: Strawberries and Brie 61

Chapter 9: Black Ribbons 73

Chapter 10: Mind-Blowing 81

Chapter 11: Epic 91

Chapter 12: Sensation 101

Until Next Time: A Note to Our Readers 111

Keep in Touch! 113

Chapter 1

THE MOST BEAUTIFUL WOMAN IN THE WORLD

He Said ...

Sitting on the edge of the bed, waiting for her to emerge from a playful and suspenseful "let-me-slip-into-something-a-little-more-comfortable" disappearance, I felt anxious in a way that still surprised me. I felt like a young groom on his wedding night or a bachelor on the proverbial third date, wondering if I'd measure up and if the fantasy and the reality might actually collide. (*They always did.*) I silenced my cell phone and set it down gently on the bedside table. I could hear faint noises of preparation coming from the bathroom ... a hairbrush being placed on the countertop, the click of what might have been the cap on a tube of lipstick, a puff of perfume being sprayed.

Then the door opened, and she walked slowly toward me, barefoot and beautiful. I was immediately transfixed by the sight of her in blue and white lingerie; the colors accentuating her milky, smooth skin made my breath hitch just a bit. "Come here," I said when she stopped just a few feet away. She crept into the space between my knees, leaning forward to kiss me as her hands found the back of my head and the edge of my jawline. She drew me gently and willingly to her. I'd always loved this first moment — touching her silky skin again, smelling her delicious body, hearing her gentle moans and whimpers and sounds of love.

She crawled onto the bed and reclined against me, letting me run my hand over her shoulder, down her arm, and through her fingers before moving it across her hip to the curve of her ass. *Velvet.* She was wearing the most exquisite velvet. Soft and thin and white, with dark blue flowers and light blue lace framing her voluptuous breasts. *My god, she was beautiful. I hope I remembered to tell her so.*

She silently moved to help me out of my shirt and free me from my pants. As she pulled them from my legs, her long strawberry-blonde hair fell forward to lightly caress my skin. Even her hair was part of the sensory experience of loving her. She knelt before me, a goddess in her lingerie, as she kissed the inside of my bare thigh, *so very close*, then licked the tip of my cock, making me suck in my breath. *Not yet. Her satisfaction comes first.*

I scooped her up and laid her softly onto the mattress as she flashed me that look she gets — the one that says, "I don't know exactly where you're taking me, but let's go."

And so we did. I slid the white velvet up over her hips to reveal nothing underneath but her gorgeous, warm body. I could have admired her all day but decided there was no time like the present to *show* her my admiration. I slid two fingers along the folds of her sex, already wet with arousal, and watched her back arch instinctively as she called out my name. *God, I loved that.* Everything about her made me wild with ecstasy — the silken ivory of her skin, the way she smelled, the way she moved beneath my hands. And, oh, the way she tasted.

Her clit grew swollen and hard at the touch of my tongue as I swirled across and around it, sucking on it before sliding down to lick along the length of her slit. She tangled her hands in my hair before letting go to grasp at the sheets with desire, splaying her arms out in stunning vulnerability.

It would be a perfect world indeed if I could do this every day — twice perhaps. Watching her tremble with pleasure, feeling my own body vibrate with anticipation and gratitude. I wanted her to feel every sensation I knew how to create ... with my tongue, my teeth, my nose, my fingers. I felt her thighs tense beneath me and knew she was surrendering to the sensation, to a climax that was awe-inspiring to watch and feel and, yes, taste.

I held her as she settled into the afterglow, kissing her forehead, and gathering her weakened limbs into my arms. I was such a lucky man, here in this moment with her, wanting for nothing. We laid like that for what might have been minutes or hours, talking and laughing and exploring with our fingers. I loved the slow pace of "after," which was almost always a sort of prelude to something more.

I could sense her energy returning as her voice became stronger and her kisses more insistent. She pushed herself up, looking sated but eager, and kissed me ... deeply, passionately. She started to twist away from me, glancing flirtatiously over her shoulder before swinging one leg over my body, straddling and presenting me with two handfuls of her curvy, succulent ass. *Is this really happening?*

Almost before I could gather my thoughts I found myself buried inside her and she slid up and down, deeper, wetter. *Yes, oh god, yes.* Her long hair was thrown back as she rocked, the loose waves falling over her shoulders while I held her hips like a desperate man on a wayward sea vessel.

She gripped at my thighs for leverage. When she rose up, I could watch my cock pulling open the slick folds of her pussy before she pushed herself back down, deeper onto the base of my cock. My abdomen and thighs were slick and shiny, and I could hear our bodies sucking and smacking together in the most salacious way. The feelings were so intense that I wanted to close my eyes and lose myself in the sensation, but I couldn't help but stare. It was the hottest thing I'd ever seen. Felt. Heard. I never imagined that my shy, sweet lover would show me a side of her that was just as beautiful and captivating as the perfect face I was already so accustomed to adoring during our lovemaking.

"Yes. Oh, god, yes."

I don't know if she said it or I did. Maybe we both did. All I know is that it was perfect. I was holding onto her hip with one hand and trailing my fingertips down her spine with the other when I knew I couldn't hold back any longer. We surely woke the neighbors when I came, crying out, clutching her — two-handed — around the waist, watching her ride through the waves of my own ecstasy.

She Said …

I'm not sure how it is that, after all these years, I still sometimes feel shy at first touch, first kiss, first naked glance. There's something special about having butterflies in your stomach for the man you love, even when he's a "sure thing" and even when you already know he adores you.

I was feeling that typical bundle of nerves and excitement — smitten like a teenager — as I was fussing with my hair and adjusting the lacy straps of the new lingerie I'd purchased for the occasion — a negligee made from thin crushed velvet in pure white, with delicate midnight-blue flowers and pale blue straps that extended down into a low, sweetheart neckline that showed all my best curves. I stood before the mirror in the powder room, wondering if he was also nervous and excited, eagerly awaiting my return. I gave myself one last glance in the mirror, smiled, and walked out into the bedroom.

He was sitting on the edge of the bed, still fully clothed in jeans and a polo shirt. I heard him sigh softly before he said, "Come here," almost a whisper. He watched me close the distance between us with silent steps on the plush carpet, never breaking eye contact.

I walked until I stood between his knees. His hands reached out for my hips and I leaned forward to kiss him, letting my loose hair cascade over his shoulders. He tasted like spearmint.

He patted the mattress, inviting me to crawl up next to him, and I did. Settled onto one hip and draped across his lap, I felt his hands drift along my spine and the soft touch of my nightie. "Velvet. I like it." He leaned over to kiss the rise of one breast, then the other. When I looked him in the eyes, I saw something I rarely take the time to see — pure awe. In that moment, I felt like the most beautiful woman in the world. *How does he do that?*

I slowly began to remove his clothes, one garment at a time, in no hurry but surely hungry to see all of him. I slipped from the edge of the bed to the floor as I freed him from his pants and boxers. *Oh, my.* I looked up at him and took a moment to kiss the inside of his thigh before licking the tip of his cock teasingly.

"Oh, god," he murmured.

Energized, he put his strong hands under my arms and lifted me back onto the bed, laying me down in one swift move and sliding the white velvet up over my hips to reveal the bare curves underneath. "Mmmm …"

Before I could take a breath, his fingertips were teasing at my clit, his tongue dancing on the inside of my thigh. I tossed my head back on the pile of pillows, my heart beginning to race and my temperature rising. "Yes …"

His tongue eagerly moved into the folds of my sex, circling my swollen clit. It was so good. *So fucking good.* I was dripping wet and could hear the delicious sound of him licking my sex, ravenous and attentive to my every whimper and wiggle. His face and hands expertly played my body to its greatest delight as I felt his tongue dip into my pussy, hot and probing, before returning to fervently suck at my clit. To my surprise, I felt his fingers slide into me … one, two, three, deeper … providing that nirvana-like combination of fucking and sucking that was so perfect. My thighs were trembling, my hands grasping at the sheets as I begged him, *yes, please, don't stop.* He rose up and I felt the cool drip of pre-cum from his hardened cock spread across my heated thighs. *Oh, god, I couldn't wait to give him this kind of pleasure too.* But I was suddenly blinded by the ecstasy of it all, lost in a place without thought, with only physical sensation and a deep sense of love and adoration. At the mercy of his skilled ministrations, my body soared into its first orgasm of the night.

He kissed my thighs and my belly and my breasts as I rocked through the beautiful aftershocks, waiting for my breathing to slow. "Hi," he said as he found my face and smiled like a man who held all the secrets of the world. Or at least those of my body and my heart.

"Lie down," I told him as I rose up to a sitting position, then onto my knees. He turned onto his back, resting his head on the pillow that had just been warmed by my own head, the very same pillow I had bitten down on in the throes of pleasure as I cried out in a way that could have woken the neighbors.

One of the best parts of making love to him is being able to look him in the eyes, to kiss him, to run my fingers and palms over his chest and nipples. So, adventurous as I may be, I often forgo experimenting with other positions. *But not tonight.* Tonight I threw one leg over his hips to straddle him backward. It only took a second for him to catch on, as he grabbed my hips from behind and helped me settle myself, slowly, smoothly, deeply, onto his cock and soak him with the warmth of my arousal. I held tightly onto his muscular thighs as I began to confidently rock against his pelvis with mounting need.

I opened my eyes just long enough to realize I was facing the mirror hanging above the dresser. *Wow, we make quite a sexy sight.* I smiled and closed my eyes again, focusing on the sensation of him moving in and out of my body, of the touch of his hands on my waist and hips and of the soft brush of my hair spilling down my back as I moved.

"I can't hold back any longer," I heard him say.

"Then don't."

And with the swiftness of a raft hitting the arc of a wave, we rose up together, bucking and rolling through his orgasm. And as always, in his deepest moment of rapture, he held onto me for dear life, firmly but lovingly, lost in the moment. Lost in us.

Time Out:
A NOTE FROM THE AUTHORS

Whew. Pretty amazing.

Do you need a breather?

We wanted to start off the book with a story that would catch your attention and make you believe — for the first time or perhaps again — in the magic that happens when love and lust aren't mutually exclusive.

But we have perhaps gotten a little ahead of ourselves. So, now we'll take you back to the beginning … to a time when our main characters (and narrators) were just coming to grips with how they felt about each other, and to the moments when they first touched and first knew that their sexual connection was the thing of fantasies and fairy tales.

This collection of stories is equal parts sultry and sweet, titillating and truthful.

Enjoy every moment, every hitched breath, every sensory detail. We hope you find it inspirational, in every possible way.

Chapter 2
VELCRO SKIRT

He Said ...

"What am I doing here?" I thought as I opened the heavy wooden door and stepped from the golden afternoon sunshine into the darkened bar. I blinked hard, instantly disoriented and waiting for my eyes to adjust. And there she was, sitting at a little table in the corner, nervously peeling the corners off a cocktail napkin. The shaft of light from the door closing behind me had caught her attention and she was looking straight at me. Her blue eyes sparkled for just a fleeting moment before the room darkened again and I took a courageous step toward her. *Play it cool.*

"Hi!" She said it with a playful lilt in her voice as she stood up to hug me, nonchalant and as naturally as if we'd been meeting for Tuesday-night cocktails for years. She looked gorgeous, but I wasn't sure if I was supposed to notice. She was curvy in all the right places and tiny inside the embrace of my hug. Her pixie haircut said *I'm low maintenance and professional*, but — honestly — when it came to what she'd been doing to my heart and mind all these years, low maintenance probably isn't how I'd describe her.

The waitress stopped by just as we were getting through the niceties about our workdays and about how glad we were to be making the time for this reunion. I ordered a Jack and Coke; she ordered something sweet that reminded me of dorm-room mixology. It made me smile.

At one point, she shifted in her seat and brought her knees out from under the table, just barely, but far enough that I saw the lacy edge of one black stocking. *What is it that's so damned sexy about silk stockings?*

"You look amazing," I said. She smiled and paid me a compliment, and then paused for just a second before telling me that her outfit was new and that the skirt wasn't really a skirt at all — that it was more of a long rectangle of fabric that wrapped around her waist and was held in place with a strip of Velcro.

A Velcro mini skirt.

Um, what did she just say? Okay, this is not my imagination.

I was clearly not the only one who went into this "cocktail date" with more than innocent nostalgia in mind. *I can't believe she said that. I can't believe I'm sitting here at a complete loss for words.*

I was instantly distracted — musing about whether she felt the same way about me as I felt about her, all these years later. She giggled to break the tension and took another sip of her drink. And, just like that, she changed the subject. She told me about an athletic challenge she was training for (a sort of quirky torture that only suburbanites could appreciate) and asked about my family. I asked some questions about her training regimen and told her she was crazy, then spoke about my kids for a while. Talking to her was so easy. It always had been.

Maybe it was the thrill of the chase — that need to be with the one woman who had gotten away — but I was pretty sure it was so much more than that. There's just something about young love, and I'm the first to admit that our star-crossed circumstances, from the very start, held a little piece of my heart.

I was so lucky to have found her again … and just a few miles down the road. *But now what?*

I didn't have the kind of wife who would be comfortable with me suddenly rekindling a friendship with an old high-school sweetheart. And the idea of being secret (*what? friends? lovers?*) was too much to think about. So, instead I thought about the shape of her lips and the way she glanced over my shoulder briefly each time the billiard balls cracked together loudly across the room or when one of the bubbas at the bar guffawed in that gonna-fall-off-my-barstool kind of way. I thought about how impossible it was that she thought she was this nerdy, understated business professional when everyone who had ever met her knew that the phrase "dead sexy" was a more fitting descriptor.

At one point, when we were talking about favorite memories, she dabbed at the table with a napkin to dry it off, then leaned her forearms onto the table and crab-walked her fingertips toward mine. I took a long, slow, deep breath in and threaded my fingers between hers. We still fit perfectly together. She smiled and crinkled her nose, just like she did when she was 14. I was done for.

I held on for a long while before giving in to the reality that was closing in around us.

"We really should get going."

I didn't want to go. But we paid the check and thanked our waitress, who winked and smiled and wished us a good night.

I held the door and let her lead the way into the moonlight. I have no idea how many hours had passed, but they had passed all too quickly. I assumed we'd hug and go our separate ways, but the parking lot was empty except for our two cars, side-by-side.

Well, wouldn't you know it? So much for a swift, casual getaway.

We walked until we were standing between her passenger-side door and my driver's-side door, listening to the crickets and marveling at the perfect weather. But I just couldn't let her go. Not yet.

Unsure even of my next moves, I stepped forward to tell her how glad I was that she asked to meet me tonight ... but nothing came out of my mouth. Instead, I put my hands on her waist and kissed her, slowly at first, then more deeply. She softened into my arms and nibbled at my bottom lip, leaning backward until the bare skin of her lower back was against the cool metal of her car. She murmured something softly that sounded like *oh my god* and kissed me back in the way I always dreamed she might.

How in the world I was going to let her go and then get into my car — alone — was beyond me. But this night had always been headed toward "goodbye" and now it was here. I wanted to turn back the clock, just a few hours, so we could do it all again.

I stepped back to admire her — the deep scoop neck of her blouse and the soft arcs of her breasts, the front of that black Velcro skirt where I'm quite sure I'd just left an indentation from my own anxious body when I pressed up against her. I saw her swallow hard and sigh. It was time.

"I'll see you soon," she said as I took just one step backward toward my truck, reaching into my pocket for the keys.

"Yes," I said. It was all I could think. All I could feel. All I had ever known since the moment I met her, all those years ago.

She Said ...

The only man I ever picked up in a bar was one I knew long before we got there.

We sat at a little two-top table in a corner, far enough away from the glow of the pool-table lights and the dart boards that it felt like dusk, and the faint orange light against his cheekbones reminded me of candlelight. I was feeling nervous. And romantic. And a little daring.

I ordered the only drink that came to mind — an amaretto stone sour — and tried to act calm and focused as I sipped it slowly and listened to him tell stories about what he'd been doing during the years we were apart. Finding him again was a gift I had yet to unwrap.

We were just friends now, really, but my outfit — carefully chosen for his benefit — telegraphed a different intention. The scoop-neck top, clinging

amazon Gift Receipt

Send a Thank You Note

You can learn more about your gift or start a return here too.

Scan using the Amazon app or visit
https://a.co/d/3zy49tK

He Said, She Said: **12 Uncensored Tales of Love and Lust (The Kiss & Tell Series)**

Order ID. 113-7478371-7068265   Ordered on September 20, 2021 in all the right places; the short black skirt; the stockings. "You look amazing," he said.

"Thanks," I smiled. Then, knowing exactly what I was doing, I told him that the skirt was new and that it was really just a length of fabric that wrapped around my waist twice and fastened with a strip of Velcro. He swallowed hard; I watched him shift in his chair.

We reminisced about high school and talked of our aspirations for the future. I wondered if there might ever be a place for me in his life trajectory, as someone more than just a memory of times past. It's all I had ever wanted … to be his for more than a moment in time. To simply be his.

The drink was sweet in my mouth. My tongue puckered with each sip, before settling into the flavor of the smooth, syrupy amaretto. If he kissed me now, he'd remember this taste forever.

But I most certainly was not going to be kissing him. This wasn't a date. It was just a chance to reflect on where we'd been. To wax nostalgic about the "good old days." At the end of the night, when our drinks were gone, we'd jump headlong back into our real lives. We'd say goodbye and tuck away the memories for another time.

I heard the murmurs of other patrons at the bar, the clinking of glasses being filled by ice. It all sounded so far away. I couldn't stop watching his every move, absorbing the tension and release of every gesture and expression. He had this way of smiling very slowly — first, just the slightest curve of his lips at the corners, then one side rose higher before his lips parted at the center to reveal just the tiniest glimpse of his straight, white teeth. And then he'd laugh or shake his head as if trying to get me off his mind … but failing miserably. *I wonder if he has any idea how sexy he is … or what he's doing to me.*

I pushed aside my cocktail glass and wiped the moisture from the table with a little white napkin so I could rest my forearms and lean closer. I wanted to give him my undivided attention, and even the act of sipping my drink had become too much of a distraction. I wanted to watch the low light glitter in his blue eyes. I wanted to remember this night forever in case I needed the memory to keep me warm when he disappeared from my life again.

He took a deep breath, letting his body relax forward against the table, and threaded his fingers through mine. I only broke his gaze to glance down at how beautiful our hands looked together.

I don't know how many hours we sat there before one of us said, "We really should get going." We had homes and people – families – waiting on us.

I didn't want to go.

But we paid the tab and walked out into the night. Our cars were parked next to each other in the adjacent parking lot and the facing street was empty — not many people stay out late at small-town taverns on a Tuesday night. The moon hung low, and the crickets were singing the kind of tune that makes you feel like your ears are buzzing. My whole body was buzzing and had hit a fever pitch by the time we made it to our cars. I found myself standing relatively still but twisting nervously on the balls of my feet, letting the high heels of my shoes sweep just millimeters above the pavement. "So …"

Neither of us wanted to say goodbye. Our story had been too much goodbye and not enough hello. And just as I was trying to think of something witty and sexy to say, he stepped closer like he was going to give me a hug. But he didn't stop there. He pressed his palm against the small of my back and gently leaned me against the side of my car to kiss me, long and slow and warm. My ears stopped buzzing and the whole world fell silent.

I put my arms around him, one on the back of his neck and the other reaching around his back, pulling him closer. *My god, he kisses like he's making love — attentive and hungry and totally lost in the moment.* (Not that I would know how he makes love, but I'd always imagined!) I could feel the evidence of his arousal pressed against me. My heart was racing.

I made a feeble attempt at a joke about the dark tinted windows of my car, knowing as soon as I said it that it made me sound like a lovesick teenager, but also suspecting he'd forgive me for the awkwardness. Because at least now he knew that he wasn't the only one overcome by desire. It was an open invitation that I hoped would stand until he was ready to say yes.

He let his forefinger slip into the waistband of my skirt, brushing along my naked hip. "Velcro, huh?" I nodded and smiled.

He shook his head and kissed me again, then let go like he'd just been pulled away by some unseen force. He stepped backward toward his truck, never once breaking eye contact with me.

"I'll see you soon," I said to reassure both of us that this wasn't goodbye. It definitely was *not* goodbye.

Chapter 3
UMBRELLA

He Said...

Being in love brings out the gentleman in me. The strong male role model in my life was my grandfather, so maybe I have some old-fashioned views on chivalry and manners. I've always said "please" and "thank you." I've always opened doors for women and held them for any person coming through.

I'm also a red-blooded male with an intense interest in the fairer sex and, in particular, my girl. She just brings out the best (and the beast) in me. By chance, we each had settled after high school in the far north suburbs of the city — near enough, in fact, to be called neighbors. When I discovered she was attending a conference in the city, it was in the spirit of being "neighborly" that I volunteered to drive her to the city on my way to work. We spent most of the ride exchanging idle chit-chat, nothing more serious than the weather and traffic. I'll admit it was nice just to have companionship for the long drive, but it was made all the better having *her* as my companion.

By the time we arrived at my office downtown, a light rain had begun, just enough to make her walk across the street to the bus stop damp and potentially treacherous. Luckily, my office building comes with a manually operated rain-deterrent device — an umbrella. I opened the door for my beautiful lady, pressed the button on the umbrella, and deftly maneuvered her under its protective fabric. As a gentleman should, I placed myself between her and the oncoming traffic. At the halfway point, I placed her on my left, one hand on her lower back, the other just overhead holding the umbrella. Our timing was excellent, as the bus arrived within seconds to whisk her off to her meetings. I raised the umbrella as I delivered a quick and impromptu kiss, held out my hand to help her up the step into the bus, and called out, "Have a wonderful day!"

The workday was a typical one for me, but I found myself looking at the clock more often than usual. I couldn't wait for her to come back. When the time finally arrived and I saw her making her way into the building, I quickly stood and made an attempt to straighten my clothes before walking out to meet her.

"Hi." She smiled, almost shyly.

"Hey there. How was your day?" I asked casually, as if I hadn't been waiting all day for just this moment.

She kind of shrugged, gave me a wink and said, "Have you ever heard this song?"

She handed me one of her earbuds as I listened intently to the music, our heads together. For the life of me, I couldn't tell you what the lyrics to the song were, but they were decidedly intimate in nature ... something about hips and butterflies. Not what I expected from her. I grinned and shook my head. Maybe it was the close proximity, maybe the explicit lyrics, or it could have been her intoxicating scent, but I found myself staring at her lush, kissable lips.

Placing both hands on her lower back, I drew her to me. My eyes slowly closed as our lips met then parted as our tongues began a slow dance. Somehow, we shuffled back to my office and I closed the door before pressing her back against my heavy mahogany desk. Her tiny hands slid under my shirt and slipped up to caress my chest. Unexpectedly, she tugged it over my head and leaned forward to lick one of my erect nipples. *This certainly seemed like an invitation!* Urgently, I pulled her top off, reached around and unclasped her bra. Stepping back, I took a deep breath, held her arms wide, and admired the glorious breasts before me.

"Oh my god, you're so beautiful." I exhaled.

I let go of her hands, overcome by the urgent need to touch her breasts. I cupped them, one in each hand, squeezing gently and raising them up, feeling their heft. As my hands slid along her smooth, porcelain skin, my thumbs grazed lightly over her nipples. With a sharp inhalation of breath, she lowered her hands and traced the contour of my hardened cock through my pants, eliciting a low moan from my throat. Before I knew what was happening, my pants were unbuttoned, the zipper lowered, and my cock was free from its confinement. She wrapped her fingers around me in a tight grip, her thumb dipping into my slippery pre-cum as she rubbed it over the head. I needed this woman. I wanted to see her entire body; I had to feel her every curve.

We tore each other's clothes off. I kissed her bare shoulders, held her about the waist, and stared longingly into her eyes. I propped her up on the desk's edge, the cool surface forcing a momentary gasp from her mouth. Her soft hands trailed simultaneously down my body and up my neck. She pulled my body closer while bringing my head down for a deep kiss. As I reached down to move my cock into place. I was surprised to discover just how wet she was.

"Oh god." I moaned as I gripped my dick and rubbed it along her opening, our juices mingling together. With every fiber of my being, I wanted this. I wanted, not to fuck her senseless, but to love her into blissful oblivion. I wanted to love her ... I was millimeters from pressing inside her and yet I hesitated.

What the hell am I doing? I thought.

"I'm sorry, we can't do this," I said straightening up. "Not like this. We deserve more. You deserve better."

She looked surprised and crestfallen. She said nothing but just stared at me — with big, concerned eyes — as if she was lost.

I knew I should have explained my thoughts more clearly. I wanted her to know that she deserved romance, candlelight, silky sheets, respect, and love — not a lusty romp against my desk! Not for our first time.

The look in her eyes said, *"Please love me. Please don't reject me."* I wanted to answer her plea, but my own disappointment and the abruptness of my withdrawal left me wordless. Her fear and confusion were heavy in the air.

Once we'd gathered our clothes and dressed, my brain cleared a bit. I did my best to assure her that I wanted her, I needed her, but that I wanted our first time to be special, not cheap. I longed to replace her worried look with the smile that charmed me every time.

"We can wait. We'll make it beautiful and special, private and romantic." There, just beginning to emerge, was the sweet grin I was looking for, slowly spreading and lighting up the room ... and my heart.

I knew it was the right decision. I wanted her to look back on our first time with happiness and love in her heart. I wouldn't be able to live with myself or feel like a gentleman if she ever looked back with regret.

She Said ...

Sometimes, it all starts so innocently. A shy glance sets the stage, a tiny kiss opens a floodgate of emotion, the gentlest friction of skin upon skin generates sparks.

And so it was that an unexpected rainstorm and a simple act of chivalry turned to a torrent of passion on a random Tuesday in the big city.

I had business that day downtown, and he offered to drive me to the city and save me from the tedium of yet another commuter train ride (old men sniffling, teenagers chewing gum, arrogant ladder-climbers talking too loudly into Bluetooth headsets). I was grateful and — though I never would have admitted it — hopeful that the time spent with him might lead, someday, to reigniting the flame that once burned so brightly between us. I kept my hands folded neatly in my lap during the drive. We talked about life and traffic and our schedules for the day.

When we arrived at his office, he told me that there was a bus that picked up just across the street that would take me to my meeting. I promised I'd be back later that afternoon. And then it started to rain.

"Here, let me," he said as he grabbed an umbrella from behind the reception desk just inside the building and walked me toward the door. With one swift movement, the umbrella was up and I was safe under its arc, listening to the raindrops *plip-plip-plipping* overhead as we glanced left, right, left again, waiting for a safe moment to cross the street. He put his hand confidently on the small of my back to guide me across the street. I shivered. *He's just being a gentleman.*

But when the bus arrived and he stepped forward to help me up the steps, he threw me off my emotional axis by leaning forward to kiss me. Just a tiny brush of his lips against mine. I looked up and he smiled. "Um ... I ..."

He smiled again and said, "Be back by 4:00."

My meetings went by in a blur. The details of who I met and what we discussed drifted away as I spent the next seven hours replaying that kiss over and over. *What did it mean? Why did it feel so very much like the first time he'd kissed me 20 years ago? Had he always been "the one"?*

When I walked back to his office that afternoon, I entered the building to find him just standing there, smiling, like he'd spent the past seven hours waiting for me and thinking about it too.

"Hi," I said nonchalantly, trying to be cool ... trying desperately not to let him know that my heart was racing. *It was just a kiss. He probably kisses all his friends.*

"Well, hello. How was your day?"

Pulling an earbud from my ear, I winked at him. "Have you ever heard this song?"

I handed him the earbud attached to my phone and pressed play. He furrowed his brow and smiled, just barely, on the right side of his mouth, holding his hand to his ear. Our heads close, tethered to one another by the cord connecting my earbuds, we listened together.

Curl your upper lip up and let me look around
Ride your tongue along your bottom lip and bite down
And bend your back and ask those hips if I can touch
Because they're the perfect jumping off point of getting closer to your ...

Butterfly. The song was called "Butterfly."

Picking up on the lyrics, he shook his head in a *what-am-I-going-to-do-with-you* gesture, and I knew. I lifted my heels off the ground and stretched up for another kiss, feeling his hand press against my back in a way that was undoubtedly more than a gentlemanly gesture.

His lips were as soft and warm as I'd remembered. He smelled like peppermint, and I could hear him inhaling slowly, confidently, like he was breathing me in, like this very moment was an act of sustaining our own lives. My hands cradled the back of his skull, fingers finding his silky-soft hair cropped short for the summer. I nibbled at his bottom lip and he pulled back for just a second to look me in the eyes and whisper, "Wow."

We stumbled, awkwardly intertwined like a four-legged creature, into his office and shut the door. The edge of his heavy wooden desk was just the perfect height for the curve of my butt to rest against. I slid my hands under his shirt and sighed. His chest was smooth and strong; I explored the sensual contours of his muscles with one hand as I pulled the shirt over his head. I licked a nipple, erect and the most perfect shade of sunset-over-the-Grand-Canyon. What a beautiful palette we made — his sun-kissed tan and my blushing ivory skin.

He lifted me onto the surface of the desk in one smooth movement, pulling my blouse off and unhooking my bra without interrupting the kiss that was making my legs weak. "Oh my god," he said as he allowed himself to step back and admire me. He cupped my breasts as I tore open the button and zipper of his jeans. There was nothing on my mind except desire. No worry about what this meant, no nostalgia for our past. Just pure love and desire, and an absolute surety that all the years I'd waited to touch him again had been worth it.

I could feel the moisture of my arousal soaking through my panties. We helped each other out of the rest of our clothes, and he took a moment to kiss my shoulders, hold my waist, and regard me like a prized trophy upon the rich wood at my back.

I couldn't keep my eyes off him. I let my hand slide down his torso to touch, teasingly at first, his stiffened cock. He moaned and I pulled him closer, gently squeezing his balls with my right hand and drawing his head toward me with my left for a deep kiss that left us breathless with passion and the belief that we couldn't possibly restrain ourselves any longer.

The cool surface of his desk was, by now, warm and damp with the sweat from our fevered bodies. I arched my back and pressed my breasts against him. We half-stood, half-laid against the desk, lost in the moment of feeling our sexes brush against each other, wet and needy. It was time … I needed to feel him inside me.

"Oh my god," I whispered.

"You're so beautiful," he said, as his eyes suddenly fell away and he straightened up his body, pulling away from our heat. He leaned over and gave me a kiss much like he had under the umbrella — delicate, soft … quick. The mood had shifted in the blink of an eye.

"We can't," he said. "Not like this. We deserve better than this. We can wait."

Confusion overwhelmed me and I felt my muscles go lax, my breathing slow. But every molecule in my body was still tingling with desire. *I don't understand.* I thought he wanted me as badly as I wanted him. "But please … no … it's okay … don't stop …"

He handed me my blouse, and I felt everything all at once: confused, hurt, sad, terrified that I had done something wrong. He was and always had been the love of my life, and the universe had finally put us in a room together again. *This was it.* Our moment to finally demonstrate how much we were meant to be together.

As if he could read the desperation in my mind, he said, "This isn't how it's meant to be. I want to make love with you on a beautiful bed in a quiet place where we have time and privacy … and romance."

And so we quietly reassembled ourselves, garment by garment, watching one another for signs of what we were feeling and where we'd go from here. We drove home mostly in silence, replaying in our minds the fire that had just burned so bright. Never had an evening commute been so full of erotic tension and emotional possibility. I tried not to sulk. I tried not to cry, but the tears brimmed as I kept the conversation light and hopeful. I kept my left hand on the inside of his thigh while he drove, my fingertips grazing his manhood ever so slightly, a sure reminder that I was still very much here and that, despite my disappointment over the abrupt end of the day's adventure, I trusted his decision. Admired it. Was grateful for it. Comforted by knowing that the sexiest man I had ever known cared enough to give me the gift of love and remembrance.

The rain had stopped and the sun was shining again. The innocence of the day had been shattered in a truly beautiful, yet irreversible way. Our relationship had broken open, vulnerable and — for the first time in years — with the promise of tomorrows. I knew then, as we approached our off-ramp and the return to our everyday lives, that I'd always feel his strong hand on the small of my back when I opened an umbrella and that my heart would race every time it rained.

Chapter 4
FINALLY

He Said ...

I've had a complicated relationship with sex. It has served many roles in my life — most of them destructive or disappointing. It has been my distraction and my pain, my weapon and my shame. A tool, an obligation, and a means to an end. I have been a body and an object of desire, as well as a man with "great skills" for satisfying the ladies.

In the end, it was me who was never really satisfied. I'd all but given up on the idea that I could have a great sex life, or that touching and being touched could be an act of *making* love — that I could give of myself and receive unconditional acceptance and desire.

Yet, in the back of my mind, all those years, there was her. She should have been my first, but she wasn't. She should have been the fairy tale, but we drifted. She should have been my second chance, but the chances came and went.

Still, I couldn't let go of the beautiful and forbidden thought — the idea of laying her down on a bed and being unapologetically me, of being vulnerable and truthful about how I've felt all these years.

We'd had some amazing moments in recent months, and it was clear that she was feeling what I was feeling. But life and commitments — and the haunting whispers of the moral majority — kept us from crossing the line. Ours was a love affair that had gone unconsummated for more years than we cared to count.

You could have knocked me over with a feather when, one day while we were chatting on the phone during our evening commutes, she said, "We should do this." I knew what she meant. *Sex. We should finally be together.* I opened my mouth and closed it. Opened it again when I realized she was expecting a response but I was still mute. I took a deep breath and finally said, "Okay. We shall." My heart was racing.

When?

Tonight? Tomorrow? Next week? Can I go through with this? Can I possibly wait another minute now that I know she'll be mine?

We made tentative plans, and then we got swept back into our "real" lives.

I didn't sleep well that week. I kept fantasizing about what she'd look like by the glow of candles, or whether her sweet, slow smile would blossom when we touched, skin-on-skin, in a way we'd never known. I was also downright terrified.

When the day arrived, I was so sure I'd say "yes" in every way, but my nerves got the best of me. By the time she called, I told her that I wasn't sure I could do this. I could picture her on the other end of the line, trying to be strong, trying not to cry. It killed me to say "no" — it killed me to break her heart (and mine). Again.

She suggested we still meet for lunch to talk it over and give ourselves some closure. She rarely took no for an answer.

At lunch, we ate sloppy sandwiches, crunched potato chips, and sipped soft drinks. It was all very casual — too casual for the importance of the discussion — and surprisingly loud. Too much music and too many other diners. I could barely focus on the small talk, much less upon what I wanted to do or say in this moment — this moment I knew would be engraved in our memories forever as a turning point (or an end).

I didn't want it to end. I couldn't let it end. *I loved her.* I had never told her as much, but she knew. She deserved to be certain.

And so lunch gave way to a little drive and an awkward conversation with a hotel desk clerk. I could barely breathe as I watched her sign the credit card receipt and smile at me with a confidence I found intoxicating.

She handed me the key.

The afternoon was a blur, but I remember the details that mattered most. Like how that first kiss felt, when I interrupted her as she was taking off her necklace and kicking off her shoes. Like the smell of her perfume when I lifted her shirt over her head. Like the sensation of her bare waist inside the circle of my arms when I came back to "rescue" her after I closed the curtains and rendered her momentarily unable to see in the sudden darkness.

I was surprised by how sure I felt, after all, when I took her hand and tiptoed us through the piles of clothing on the floor. I looked back over my shoulder at her and smiled as she crinkled her nose, raising her cheekbones high as she stood in a sliver of light that peeked through the shuttered windows.

I set her gently on the end of the bed, cradling her head as I laid her down. *My god, she was beautiful.* I couldn't help but stare. At her narrow shoulders and her ample breasts, tipped in pink. At the curve of her hips and the soft fluff of strawberry-blonde hair across her pubic bone, hiding the treasure beneath.

I was still staring when she reached up to run her hands down my chest. I shivered. Leaning up, she kissed me furtively and then reached down to wrap her hands around my cock, at full attention and longing for her. One lick … a sort of promise.

I touched her breastbone softly but firmly, urging her back onto the mattress, and I dropped to my knees. Every inch of her smelled delicious — clean and floral and impossibly brand new. I kissed her knees and her thighs, her belly and her hips, before nestling the tip of my nose into that fluff of hair and inhaling deeply. She smelled like love and desire. It was exactly as I had always imagined.

The sounds of her accelerated breathing and soft moans drove me forward as I separated the folds of her flesh to reveal the slick pink perfection of her sex. She tasted as delicious as she smelled. I couldn't get enough as my tongue tickled her clit to swollen erection. She writhed on the bed, whimpering my name, and sounding somehow both desperate for more and completely satisfied. I let my hands and mouth explore every bit of her, thinking I could love her like this for hours if she'd let me.

Our bodies were getting warmer and her writhing gave way to trembling. I could feel every muscle in her thighs begin to tighten and twitch … a sort of preamble to the rolling thunder of the orgasm that was rising up within her.

"Oh, god … don't stop … it's so … so … ohmygod …"

Her back arched and her chin pointed to the ceiling before rolling to the side as she clutched the bedding with her fists and bit the pillow. She was so beautiful. She had always been so very beautiful.

I watched her in awe as she lay there with her eyes closed for a full minute or two. Then I helped reposition her and laid down, scooping her into my arms where she belonged. She kissed me in a delicate, tired way that felt like gratitude and love and coming home.

"I …" I began but couldn't find the words. She smiled and closed her eyes for just a moment. I closed mine too. We remained still while our breathing slowed and our bodies cooled — while my brain caught up with my heart, trying to comprehend what it meant when the woman of your fantasies is suddenly and perfectly your reality. I had never felt so fortunate in my life. *Did I deserve this?*

I kissed her, looking down to find her no longer tired and dreamy but alert and ready. It was finally *our* time.

I sat up, elevating myself over her on the bed. As I leaned forward to kiss her again, she reached up and wrapped her arms around my neck, breathing in my own scent, hungrily, peppering my shoulders with kisses and licks and tiny nibbles. I couldn't believe she wanted this as badly as I did. Wanted *me*. Not just for the diversion or the release or the entertainment that sex can offer. She wanted *us*. And I did too. The universe had been conspiring, year after year, reunion after reunion, coincidence after coincidence to make this day possible. *We deserved this.*

I found her hands with my own, pressing my palms into hers, lacing our fingers together as I pinned her to the mattress and gave her one last, innocent kiss. With our hands framing the spill of her long hair upon the sheets, we came together at last. I slid smoothly into her warmth, feeling a kind of ecstasy I'd never experienced before. "Oh my god …" I whispered, as her breath hitched in the back of her throat. I thought I might die from satisfaction and relief.

As I began to move inside her, her body gripped mine tightly, igniting my every neuron. The world fell silent and peaceful while our bodies fell into a sensual dance, slow at first, building rhythm as our bodies sang together. In, out. Yes, more. Deep, deeper. She hungrily quickened the pace, rocking me with her thrusts, wrapping her arms around my back to gain purchase. Our eyes locked and she smiled, seeming to nod almost imperceptibly as my orgasm rose and shot through me. I threw my head back as I sunk as close and deep inside her as I ever dreamed. *This.* This was worth waiting for. This impeccable moment of love and lust, where nothing else mattered except me and her and this gift we gave one another. Words were unnecessary as years of untold love and longing sprang forth in the single sparkling tear that I kissed from the corner of her eye.

She Said …

In life, there are fantasies and there are dreams. And this day was a dream come true.

He was my first love. The first man who made my heart race; the first slow, coy smile that turned me inside out; my first kiss; my first instinct that I might be beautiful or desirable. But back then, we were just teenagers, and life was full of powerful forces that would continually pull us apart. We grew up. We grew away.

But we never forgot. Decades after those sweet childhood longings, we found each other again. And somehow, we had the courage to talk about what could have been. I wished he had been my first. He wished I had been his. We were grateful beyond measure that the universe had brought us back in touch again.

I was awe-struck by how much my longing for him had grown over the years. And the reality of him today — muscular and confident and eloquent about his feelings — was almost too much to bear. I knew the moment I saw him that it wasn't too late to fall in love again, that the time had finally come to consummate what we'd started all those years ago.

So, we flirted and talked. We went Christmas shopping together, letting our hands touch briefly while we discussed the merits of stocking stuffers, and we shared countless lunches and winks and flirtatious jokes.

"We should do this," I said one day, months after reuniting. We were on the phone and I could actually feel the emotional tension on the line as he took a breath. "Okay. We shall," he said.

So we took the afternoon off from work and agreed to meet at a hotel. As my turn signal clicked and I took the last highway exit before our destination, my phone rang. "I'm not sure I can do this."

My heart leapt into my throat. I had waited 20 years to be held in his arms against the sheets. I had dreamt of him every night for weeks on end, replaying comments he'd made, like the afternoon I stopped by his workplace and he touched the ends of my strawberry-blonde hair and said, "Wow. It's getting so long. I bet it looks beautiful on a pillowcase." (*How does he do that? Act, all at once, so very sweet and so very sultry?* And it's not bravado or false charm. It's just what two people do when they have been smitten for as long as they can remember.)

"Oh," I said into the phone, belying my emotional distress. The panic had risen in my chest. I thought I was losing him. *What had I done wrong?*

"Well, I'm here. I'm down the street from your house. Can we at least meet for lunch? To talk?"

And he agreed. Perhaps reluctantly. I saw him pull his car into the parking lot by the sandwich shop and we went inside, both acting a little shy and awkward, and not at all hungry — at least not for food.

At first, we focused on our sandwiches and our chips, glad to see one another but not sure what to say. And then I reached across the table and just set my hand on top of his. He was so warm, so calm. Simmering. I couldn't tell what he was thinking or feeling, but I took a chance.

I stared at our hands, then wiggled my fingers between his and stared some more. "It's just skin."

"What?" He furrowed his brow.

"Sex. It's just skin upon skin. It's not scary or shameful or even particularly complicated. It's just me and you, like we've always dreamed it could be."

"You make it sound so simple," he said. "But it's complicated. My life … your life … the separate worlds we live in."

Please, no. I didn't want to talk him into doing something he'd regret, but I was terrified he'd leave that restaurant two steps ahead of me and never look back. We had come so far together — our friendship, our romance. *Didn't we deserve this?*

Something shifted in the air and, before I could register what had transpired, we were rising to our feet and making our way into the parking lot, into two separate cars, and weaving our way through traffic to the nearest hotel. In the left turn lane, I watched him in my rearview mirror, wishing I could read his mind. *Follow please. Please keep following me. It's going to be okay. It's going to be perfect.*

At the reception desk, I did all the talking and he hung back, like the hotel employees might call our families and friends if they got a good look at him. I took the keycard and led the way. Room 113.

I was kicking off my shoes when I heard the lock click. My nerves had gotten to me and I was fidgeting to fill the awkward silence — removing my earrings, fiddling with my cell phone — anything to avoid seeing potential regret on his face. He sauntered across the room and stopped me with a kiss.

Hard. Warm. Deep. My racing heart instantly began to slow. *I am safe. I am loved. This is our moment.*

He pulled my stretchy black and silver T-shirt over my head and sighed. I could feel the rhythm of my breathing match his own as he kissed the tops of my breasts, then my neck. He lost himself in the moment, just briefly, then pulled away. He said, "hang on" and went to the windows to draw the shades. I made a silly comment about whether there were people in the parking lot, hoping to get a free show. He chuckled and it sounded nice, comforting.

I stood completely still as my eyes adjusted to the sudden darkness in the room. "I can't see you!" I laughed. He put his arm around my bare waist and there he was again, despite his own nerves, letting me know it was going to be alright.

We shed the remainder of our clothes, slowly and somewhat awkwardly. I marveled at the musical sound of his belt buckle falling open under my fingers, the innocence of the denim against my hands as it gave way to his hot, sexy skin. I could feel his heart beating when I placed my palms against his chest. I stood on my toes and kissed him. His lips were so soft, so welcoming. We tasted like spearmint. Maybe it was his breath mint; maybe it was my Chapstick.

He walked me backward toward the bed and set me on the edge delicately. I was wearing nothing at all, and for the first time in my entire adult life, I wasn't at all self-conscious about my body. I felt as beautiful as he appeared to see me.

He laid me down and kissed every inch of me, savoring each nipple, licking a trail down my stomach toward my inner thighs. I gasped and arched my back. I leaned up to offer a sensual greeting, running my hands over his abdomen, gently stroking his beautiful cock, musing that he was as handsome and perfectly made as I had always dreamed.

"Uh-uh," he shook his head. "You first."

He pushed me back down and dipped his fingers into my wet, waiting body. *Oh my god. I can't believe this is actually happening.*

I tried, and I succeeded, to shut off the rest of my thoughts. I surrendered to what I was feeling in the moment, in my body and in my soul. I was feeling love, and it felt like nothing I had felt before.

With the most dexterous movements and perfectly timed moans, he navigated his way around my body with his tongue and his hands. My eyes, having adjusted to the dimly lit room, were transfixed upon his strong arms, the muscles tensed as he held my thighs and then my hips. His short brown hair, always perfectly cut, looked so impossibly beautiful above my sex as I began to grind and meet him, thrust for lick, moan for moan. I was going to come. He was going to catch me when the world fell away.

My god, it was so perfect. The explosion of sensation, stars in my eyes as they rolled back in pleasure, the aftershocks where he cradled my back with his palms. He smiled and I closed my eyes, letting my body feel it all and giving myself the time to properly recover.

I reached up and kissed him with all the fervor of my devotion and appreciation. I tasted myself on his lips, sweet and warm and slick. *I love you* — it didn't need to be said, but I felt it so profoundly and hoped he did too.

I shifted onto my side, touching his chest and staring at him like I was seeing him for the first time.

Finally. We were here, together, finally. And he was done waiting.

He pushed me — with confident but gentle fingertips — back down onto the bed, pinning my hands to the sheets beside my head. He fit his hips and muscular thighs so perfectly between my legs, and at last I felt the extraordinary, blissful sensation of him penetrating my sex, sliding into me, filling me. My breath hitched. I felt tears inexplicably pooling at the outer edges of my eyelids, tears of happiness and relief and utter satisfaction. I had no idea that two bodies coming together like this could be as spiritual as it was physical. *And, oh, the physical.* He paused with the kind of restraint I'd seen him exercise just one other time, on a rainy day in the city, and he stared at me and smiled. Then he thrust himself hard into me. Deep, and I let out a little cry of ecstasy.

It took me a moment to process all that I was feeling ... to remember that lovemaking took two of us and that I couldn't just watch and feel and marvel. I needed to show him how good this felt, how very much I loved him, how he had been well worth the wait despite all the years and challenges. And so I did. I wrapped my arms around his back and dug my fingertips confidently into his sides. I arched up for a hot, frantic kiss and pressed myself harder into him, drawing him deeper inside and then pulling back, gripping every inch of him with my hungry sex. I could feel our sweat mingling as he uttered a desperate and vulnerable "oh god, yes" and I felt his cock begin to throb deep inside me, pulsing his release. My body clung to him through his spasms until I felt his kisses return to my shoulders and neck and jawline and we collapsed onto the mattress, skin on skin, as we were always meant to be.

"Wow." I think we said it at the same time, otherwise speechless, and both still not quite sure why there were tears in our eyes.

Chapter 5
CHEEKY PANTIES

He Said ...

Few things are as rewarding as living out a lifelong dream. The feelings one gets from striking the game-winning hit, being an unexpected hero, or writing the next Great American Novel are seldom duplicated and rarely exceeded. Unless of course, you're speaking in the realm of fantasy. Fantasies live in a separate corner of our mind, a dimly lit corner where our secret desires are hidden from others and, occasionally, even from ourselves. Here are our visions of being that superhero, a knight fighting dragons, a space explorer in a starship in a distant galaxy.

In my corner sat a box, dusty save for the finger-polished clasps that held it closed. This was my box of carnal fantasies and I knew that, once it was opened, the lusty pandemonium unleashed would know no bounds. In these moments, I knew I was incredibly lucky to be in love with a woman who had found the key to that box, who was more than willing to open it and indulge my innermost desires.

And yet she never failed to surprise me. I had never met a more sensual woman in my life — the kind of woman who could harden my cock with a simple turn of her head. With a single look, a subtle smile, she could promise endless delight. This day, though, there was something extra behind that smile.

The last time I saw her, we were attending a business event; she was with her colleagues and I was with mine. We were separate but still titillated by being "together" in public. I caught her eye from across the lobby and waved as I approached. She winked at me and smiled, then went right back to chatting up the salt-and-pepper-haired executive who looked like just another one of her adoring fans ("I really admire your work," I could practically hear him saying. "I heard you speak last year at the pre-conference workshop …"). It was mid-morning at a bustling conference center, and she was her "everyday self" — analytical, controlled, and measured. Corporate-ladder climbers were exchanging business cards and confidently shaking packets of sugar at the coffee/tea station before the next general session.

I finally closed the gap between us on that giant expanse of gaudy hotel carpeting, shook her hand, and said something decidedly more "suitable for work" than what I was thinking. I felt like the luckiest bastard in the world — boasting silently and anonymously in my mind about being the only man at this event who know what she looked like underneath that skirt. I wished her luck during her presentation and excused myself to go find a seat. She said "thank you," leaned in to give me a business-appropriate kiss on the cheek, then whispered, "Celebrate my success on Friday?" She straightened her posture and grabbed her leather file folio and her coffee cup as I swallowed hard and said, "Count on it."

And now, here we were. It was Friday and she wasn't wearing a business suit or heels. I noticed she wasn't wearing her wedding ring either. I loved the courage in that. Without realizing it at first, I spun my own gold band with the tip of my thumb. I took a few more steps into the hotel room, acutely aware that every nerve in my body was on high alert. When she looked up and her shimmering lips spread into that smile, innocence tinged with sin, my knees went weak. "Hello, handsome," she whispered as she leaned in for a kiss. "Mmm. Hello, baby." I placed soft, gentle pecks along her lips, tracing their outline before diving into the warm, wet embrace of her mouth. Oh, how her kisses took my breath — and inhibitions — away.

Her inhibitions were gone as well. That controlled, analytical, measured, take-charge-and-take-the-stage professional persona had softened into my romantic lover. With the click of the lock behind me, she became sensual, fun, carefree, and willing to be free of control. It was intoxicating to see how she could surrender to me in a way she never surrendered anywhere else in her life. Her hands slipped down the back of my arms to my hands, grasping them softly. Slowly, she pulled me into the room, leading me to the bed. Extending her arms as she held my hands in hers, she rewarded me a mouth-watering view of her curves in lingerie. Her pale, smooth breasts spilled out from a black satin bra, trimmed with pink lace. Her skin glistened in the dim light as if dusted in fairy magic. My eyes roamed down to her panties. *Oh my, I've never seen the likes of these before.* A small triangle of material covered the delicious treasure of her sex, while the sides gave way to a wide band of lace wrapping around and dipping between her ass cheeks, concealing oh so very little.

"Do you like it?"

Do I?

"I love it."

Slowly, she let go of my hands and began a languorous spin, pausing with her back to me. Inhaling sharply, I took in the most amazing sight: the soft pale globes of her cheeks outlined by delicate lace. As if in a trance, I found my hand running down the exposed skin of her shoulders, light fingertips tracing the sides of her bra until they settled on the soft curves of her waist. I paused, once again taking in the warmth of her flesh as it sent lightning racing through my nerves straight to my cock. I kissed her spine. She shivered.

"Cheeky panties." She said with a flirtatious flip of her hair as she crawled like a vixen onto the bed before her. "Indeed," I responded, though my breath was still caught in my throat. Leaning down onto her elbows, she presented her scantily clad ass to me, high and inviting. I gawked as I eagerly pulled off my clothes, hands shaking with desire. I pressed my hands into her silken calves, massaging, caressing, sliding up the backs of her thighs to her exposed cheeks. I leaned forward and pressed my lips against the lacy fabric barely covering her skin. Her sweet scent, mingled with the lighter floral of the fabric and the intoxicating, unmistakable aroma of her arousal gathering below, drove me forward in a barely contained frenzy of lust and excitement.

I hooked my fingertips into the wide waistband of those oh-so-sexy panties and slowly drew them down her flesh. Licking a wet trail across the newly presented skin, I dipped my tongue into that sensual valley between her cheeks. I could hear her breath becoming shallower. I could feel her body responding to me. As I continued to pull her panties down her thighs, this goddess before me gracefully stretched out one leg, then the other, allowing me to free her from the garment. I placed my hands firmly upon each of her cheeks and greedily massaged her, kneaded the smooth, unblemished skin, revealing more and more of her sumptuous flesh. My body was on autopilot as my mind swirled with the possibility of another fantasy about to be fulfilled.

I pushed my tongue deeper into the cleft of her ass — long, slick laps, quick-flicking licks, combining to draw out exquisite carnal moans from her throat. Slowly, with purpose driven by desire, I circled her forbidden rosebud with the tip of my tongue, listening for any sign of hesitance from my lover. Hearing gasps of surprise and sighs of contentment, I swirled ever closer, my mouth watering, coating her with slippery wetness. My left hand moved to her eager pussy, her slick arousal coating my fingertips as they sought out her swollen clit. Simultaneously, my tongue reached her tight, textured hole as my fingers began to roll over her other sensitive bud. Her head whipped upward and her back arched with bliss. I felt my pre-cum trickling down the sensitive underside of my cock. The sensory overload drove me beyond control. Tongue lapping across her puckered entrance, fingers stroking, rubbing her clit, juices flowing from her pussy as cum leaked from my cock, I ravished her.

I pointed my tongue, exploring deeper and deeper the wonderful, rare treat that was her ass. My love bucked and thrashed against my tongue and fingers, desperately seeking release as I relished the moment of realizing my fantasy. I used my tongue on her ass as I would her pussy and clit. Alternating the long slow strokes with quick flicks and probing exploration, adding swirls and twirls and other flourishes any oral connoisseur should know. My fingers danced across her erect clit, circling, rubbing, drawing out the long-sought release she craved. With a gasp, a shout, and a throaty growl, she came hard, collapsing onto the bed in fevered exhaustion.

I slowed my attack, easing her back into the world with a flurry of kisses upon the now-rosy cheeks of her bum, cooling her with gentle caresses on the backs of her thighs until she found her breath.

"Thank you, baby. That was amazing," I said as my nose grazed her lower back.

"Mmhmm," she managed.

"You'll need to wear those more often." One wink, one smile. Just like in that conference center lobby, where the seed of today's adventure was first planted.

She Said ...

A long time ago, I thought I was a prude — a woman repressed, uptight, a real goody-goody, and a puritan. I was once shy in the bedroom, given to routine and opting almost always for romance over lust. And then I learned a thing or two about the malleability of inhibitions when they come up against the right circumstances and the right lover. I learned that love and lust can co-exist. That they inspire the best in us, in fact, when they *do* co-exist.

I've come to believe that a woman's inhibitions in the bedroom are often a reflection of a seemingly antiquated self-consciousness. It isn't an absence of adventure or a lack of passion; it's about years of cultural messaging that has told them that their bodies aren't sexy enough or thin enough or fit enough. Build her up, men, and watch her walls come crumbling down.

Case in point: My lover's obsession with my ass. *Why on earth does he want to caress it? When he's back there, looking at my curves, doesn't he see the dimples and rolls in all the wrong places? Is he judging me?*

It took me years to understand, to believe, that he actually admired me. Worshipped me. Loved every inch and arc, kissing my contours and holding me tight at the very seat of my body, just inches from my hot, tingling sex. That he was as hungry for me as I was for him. And — something that is often overlooked — that I didn't have to love asses, or even love my own ass, to appreciate that he truly does. So I had learned to watch him closely for signs of arousal at the most unsuspecting times. And I had learned to dress for the occasion.

We had recently had the rare opportunity to attend the same large professional event — one of those three-day marathons of grip-and-grin and keynote after keynote. I was in my element, as I always am when I'm working or networking. I was in control and very much in charge, mingling at the cocktail mixers and asking intriguing questions every time someone passed me a microphone. No one would have ever guessed that when I took off the skirt and heels, and found myself alone with my lover, I was able to shed the poise and leadership air for something decidedly more submissive. In the real world, I trusted myself. In his world, I trusted him.

So when I saw him crossing the lobby during the refreshment break before my big presentation, I felt a sort of power in knowing that the hundreds of people between us, rushing to grab a beverage or return a phone call or shake another hand, had no idea that hotel *rooms* (not hotel ballrooms) were more our thing. I winked and smiled, and continued listening as attentively as I possibly could to the gentleman who had just approached me to introduce himself and offer a business card. As my love approached, I lifted my chin just a bit and beckoned him into the conversation — introducing the two men with casual politeness then nodding to let my new friend know that I was going to go get ready for my speech.

Realizing our time was brief, my lover stole a warm hug and wished me luck. "Thank you," I said, holding his gaze in a way that telegraphed far more than workplace collegiality. I kissed him quickly on the cheek and whispered, "Celebrate my success on Friday?" And then I gave him a crooked grin, grabbed my presentation notes and coffee cup from the table, and walked away ... knowing full well he was watching my ass the entire time that I made my way to the stage.

Come Friday, I had all but forgotten the mundanities of work and was hungry for a few hours of mid-day lovemaking. And still eye-rolling over his obsession with my ass but accepting the compliment as it was, I decided to show him some of my best assets. My latest lingerie purchase was nothing short of stunning — a black satin bra trimmed with pink lace and matching, lacy, cheeky panties that quite literally put my ass on display. I was wearing these, and nothing else, when I opened the door to our hotel room to welcome him in.

We kissed like we were taking a long drink after a hike through the desert. We tasted each other, and I left sensory love notes across his lips, his tongue, his cheek, his neck. We'd said little other than "hello." There was simply no need, no time, no breath.

What I needed was him. I took his hands and pulled us backward toward the bed, smiling when I noticed the tented sign of his arousal. He had come from work wearing a gray suit and tie — all business — but now I knew his body was focused on an altogether different kind of business. He stared at me like I was the most beautiful woman alive. And in that moment, I believed him.

I twirled around to show off my new undergarments. As he leaned down to capture my lips, I deftly began to remove pieces of his clothing — jacket, tie, shirt, pants ... and boxers. *Oh my.* I never grew tired of seeing his cock burst free from his clothes. Hot and hard and smooth. This was the stage where we both gave our best performances.

I wanted so badly to fall to my knees and take him into my mouth, but I had a plan and didn't want to lose focus. He hooked his fingers into the waistband of my panties, eager to remove them and get straight to the business of ravishing me. *But I needed him to know. I wanted him to know that today was the day.*

"Wait," I said, stopping his hand with my own. I began to turn away from him slowly, glancing back at him over my shoulder and smiling. "Cheeky panties." I welcomed his gaze on my behind, imagining his delight at seeing my curves fully exposed below the pink lace. I crawled seductively onto the bed, shaking and presenting my ass to him as if it were a gift. I knew this was one of his fantasies, and I knew I was the lucky woman who got to help him live out his dreams and desires.

He inhaled sharply and let out a combination of words and moans that were barely perceptible.

I knew he must be close to exploding with anticipation, but as usual, he exhibited heroic restraint, taking the time to kiss and caress my body, to admire me slowly. I rested on my elbows with my ass in the air, basking in the glow of his appreciation. I felt the satin and lace start to slide over my hips and down my thighs. He was finally ready for his gift. I helped him free my legs from the panties, smiling because I knew they had served their purpose. I was surprised to feel something new well up in my chest that felt warm and safe — the comfort of surrendering to the kind of trust that had been earned over time. I knew I was safe in his hands. His strong, loving hands. I slowed my breath. Stopped being in charge for once.

When I sensed his tongue dancing along my lower back and dropping into the crevice below, I shivered. I chased away my insecurities about this new experience and focused on the sensation — his tongue warm as it slid over and around my most private part. I began to lose myself in the sounds of his desire and in the knowledge that no other woman would bring him as much joy as I do. *Oh god.* Just being touched by him, even in new ways that made me a little nervous, was utterly intoxicating.

In my surrender, I knew that he was loving every moment of this. I trusted him, knowing that the surest way to turn his fantasies into my own was to *believe* him. If he thought I was sexy, then I was. If he thought I looked and smelled and tasted delicious, then I did.

I felt his tongue press against that forbidden pucker of my skin, eagerly testing the limits of my flesh. I was surprised to find that it felt … good. Different. Sexy. Never one to ignore my needs while basking in his own heady fantasies, he slid one hand around my hip and found the wet inner sanctum of my pussy. My knees nearly gave way with the double assault, the simultaneous penetration of his fingers in front and the insistent laving of his tongue in back. I was dripping in our mingled juices. It was unlike anything I'd ever felt.

Neither of us could contain ourselves much longer. I felt my body contracting inward, the muscles preparing for orgasm, and my ears began to buzz with the overload of sensation. I was falling down a long tunnel of ecstasy, his fingertips sliding expertly in and out of my pussy and across my clit, his right hand grasping my ass, and his lips hungrily kissing and licking me in ways I'd never imagined. I cried out in such satisfaction that

I surely became the talk of the hotel. But the world outside our room simply didn't exist as he cradled me in his arms, and as my body twitched its way through the aftershocks of pleasure, and as we both murmured "I love you ... oh my god, I love you" again and again.

Chapter 6
TRUST

He Said...

We've all heard the saying, "Trust isn't given; it's earned." I couldn't agree more. It's a product of everyday interactions and routines: being honest and attentive, caring and kind, and having open conversation. Never is trust more necessary than when we're at our most vulnerable. When we're exposed and intimate and relying on the knowledge that our partner will always have our best interests in mind. Or, as was the case on this night, having her ultimate pleasure in mind.

Our lovemaking is never vanilla even when it's simple and sweet. Even the tried-and-true missionary position tends to have more sizzle for us. Perhaps it's because we experience it in a fully heightened way. There are sounds to be lost in, aromas to enjoy, sights to behold, sensations to savor, tastes to devour, and the more ephemeral senses of passion, love, lust, and, of course, trust.

I'm a sensory-driven man, and always take the time to admire her sensual beauty. She's gorgeous beyond compare with her long, golden hair tinged with red. Her expressive eyes, deep and liquid, set in a porcelain complexion, flawless, smooth, and soft. Her lips are alluring and kissable. Her taste is often of mint. Her teeth, white and gleaming, shine when she gifts me with her smile. I get lost just looking at her.

That night was no different. I admired the way her neck gently swooped down to her upper chest, leading to the curves of her voluptuous breasts. My hands made the journey from her defined jawline, down the front of her neck to the swells and peaks of her nipples. My body flooded with endorphins as my fingertips lightly trailed along the sides of her breasts to the rosy pink of her areolas, tracing teasing circles around them. I listened for her inhalation of breath before lowering my moistened lips to her skin. I licked each peak before leaning back to blow cool, focused breaths through pursed lips, stiffening her nipples to full excitement. I alternately sucked one then the other into my mouth, my palms smoothing a path around to her back and down to her lush ass. I caressed and kneaded, squeezing and releasing each cheek while continuing to lavish attention on her breasts. I wanted her to feel so many different sensations at once.

I could hear music playing in the living room and a *pop-pop-fizz* sound of coffee percolating in the kitchen. Her home was always ready for guests. I hoped I was the only guest she ever invited into the bedroom.

I kissed a slick trail with my lips and tongue down her belly, where the wonderful scent of her skin began to mingle with the aromatic juices of her sex. My mouth watered in anticipation of that sweet nectar awaiting me. I barely had enough time to admire the soft fuzz of her mound before she parted her lower lips with her fingers and revealed the pink petals within. She was breathing deeply in anticipation. My arms wrapped around her thighs, my hands gripping the tops of her upper legs. I sucked on her inner thigh, moving ever closer, closer. My lips brushed lightly against her as I continued along her opposite leg. "Please?" she asked, unable to withstand the teasing.

She was impossible to deny. "Please" was all I needed. I moved to suck her flushed outer folds. Gently, I drew them into my mouth, feeling their texture against my tongue. I searched for her slick, inner lips and ran my tongue along them with small flicks and circles, before dipping my tongue into her wet passage. Her taste was incomparable — sweet, an exotic candy with subtle, tangy notes. And it was all mine. I allowed myself time to play and enjoy the sounds of her breathing, her moans, and the occasional, "Yes, baby. Right there. Just like that." I relished the sensual sucking and licking sounds of my attentions while I surreptitiously reached over to grab a black, satin bag from the bedside table. *Oh, my love, I have a surprise for you,* I thought to myself.

While I tongue-fucked my lady to moaning delight, I pulled her favorite toy from the bag. I had seen the toy before, in titillating private photographs, but had never held it in my hands until now. It was a dildo, about eight and a half inches long and made of thick glass with a textured surface. It was cool to the touch, which I imagined would provide a delightful sensation upon her heated skin. She didn't know what was coming. With a final drag of my tongue along her sugary sweet canal, I took the slender tip of the dildo and gingerly drew it through her slippery folds until it reached her clit.

She inhaled sharply and gasped, "Oh!" I drew small circles around her sensitive button, then turned my focus directly upon its glistening surface. I was mesmerized watching the toy slide through her flushed folds, the bud of her clit slightly magnified by the curves of the nearly transparent glass.

The act of surprising her — of pleasuring her with something new — excited me. She was nearly breathless, moaning and offering high-pitched "mmms" of delight. I slid the dildo down through her juices and slid it slowly, teasingly, into her body. *Oh my.* The view of her pussy expanding to accept the glass cock and watching it disappear into her dark passage sent a rush of lust through my body as my own cock began to drip. Hearing her shallow, rapid breaths followed by rising cries of "Oh ffuuck!" My heart pounded as I realized this was a first for me, that she trusted me to give her this pleasure … it was all almost too much.

I needed more, though, just as I knew she craved a release. I worked the toy in as deeply as I dared. I paused and spun it within her, the curves of the toy stimulating her deepest sensitive spots. I paid rapt attention to the noises she was making. Hearing pleasure, I began to retract. *The way her body clung to it!* Her fluids coated the surface of the glass as it emerged, and I became hungry to taste her. I licked the exposed shaft, flooding my mouth once again with her deliciousness before returning the toy to her folds. I began to slowly piston the dildo inside her while my tongue sought out and ravished her clit. She was delirious with the combined sensations of stimulation on all parts of her sex. I pumped faster. I licked harder, pushing her to her long-awaited finish.

She began to buck her hips and I knew we were close. Her back arched, her hands grasped at her breasts, and she cried out as she crested that peak of ecstasy. But I was not done with her. I continued to suck her clit and thrust the rod into her as another orgasm exploded through her body. She clenched her entire body at once as if in shock, teetering on the brink of going mad with pleasure. *Finally! Gorgeously.* And with a great gasp, she tumbled over the edge into the valley of recovery, her breath slowing, her body quakes subsiding.

Never before had I been so awash in emotion, sound, scent, sight, taste, and touch. Never before had I been so blessed by love, lust, and trust. Why had our lives unfolded this way, where our truest selves were only stirred and unleashed in stolen moments like this? I tried not to get lost in the "what ifs" and focused instead on getting lost again in her.

She Said ...

No matter how long you've been in love (and lust), it never hurts to plan a little adventure or give the gift of surprise. That's why I love indulging in new experiences that create indelible memories. Whether it's romantic lighting, jaw-dropping lingerie, a bottle of massage oil, or a new game, I try my best to contribute a little variety and spice into our lovemaking. He's a master with the details too, which is one of the many things I adore about him.

But on this particular night, my surprise for him turned into *his* surprise for me.

I flitted around my house, waiting for him to arrive, full of nervous and playful energy. I turned on some soft jazz (deciding it was good background music for lovemaking but knowing he'd surely comment, "That's not *real* jazz"). I silenced my phone and paced the front room. I adjusted and readjusted the skinny, black ribbons between my shoulder blades, which held my bright-pink, satin lingerie perfectly in place. I turned down the bed. I checked myself in the mirror more times than was necessary. On a whim, I pulled out my satin bag of sex toys and placed it gingerly on the bedside table, thinking that it might be fun to use toys to expand our experiences. I kept all the toys and titillating goodies hidden most days, taking them out surreptitiously the moment my husband's airplane was wheels-up on its way to his next business destination. There were two men in my life; one who shared my everyday world and one who worshipped me ... body, heart, and soul.

When I heard my lover at the door, I ran downstairs to greet him. He was fumbling with his keys and cell phone, removing his suit coat and loosening his tie when I appeared, barefoot, and wearing just enough to make him drop his keys. "Well, hello ..."

I smiled and helped him finish removing his tie.

"Let's go upstairs." I excitedly grabbed his hand, lacing his fingers between mine and led him up the steps. I never glanced back but relished in the knowledge that he was watching my every curve as I sashayed toward the bedroom. I knew this was one of his very favorite views.

As I helped him remove the rest of his suit, I nodded toward the bag on the bedside table. "I thought we might be able to use a few things for inspiration." He grinned. "Hmm ...," shaking his head at me as if to say, *"Always full of temptation and surprises, my dear."*

But the moment he laid me on the bed, all thoughts of the toys in the bag escaped me. He grasped my jaw, passionately but delicately, between his hands and kissed me like it was all he'd thought about all day. *My god, I loved him.* Expecting him to join me on the bed, I closed my eyes and felt him settle between my legs. *Oh, yes ...*

He positioned my legs over his shoulders and began to kiss my inner thighs, pressing them further apart and coming closer and closer to his intimate destination. Knowing he was watching, listening, breathing me in, I wanted to show him how welcome he was in this place. With one hand, I reached down to spread open the folds of my pussy. I heard him moan. Leaving my fingers pressed against my own moist flesh, I summoned him with words and whimpers, begging him to devour me. "Mmmm ..." he muttered before losing himself in my body, licking and sucking and exploring every dripping curve. He was a master of his craft, and I was twisting with delight. "Yes! Oh, god. Yes. Don't stop ..." I wanted him inside me, on the bed, enveloping my entire body, kissing me as he slid his cock where his mouth had just been.

"Please ..." I begged.

He kept teasing and playing, and I had gathered the sheets into knots with my fists. It was delicious. It was maddening. I was fully immersed in the sensation of his hands and lips and tongue teasing me to great delight when ... *Oh!* My hot, slippery sex was suddenly bathed in something cold — deliciously and unexpectedly cold — and smooth as it slid through my folds. *What in the world was he doing?*

The rational woman inside my head was distracted and captivated by the mystery of what could possibly be creating these sensations. I started to open my eyes and curl my spine ever-so-slightly forward to see what had changed, but the woman in me who loved new experiences and who loved and trusted this man won out. This was his surprise for me, and I trusted him enough to maintain the mystery. I relaxed back on the bed and decided to surrender to the moment, to the delicious feelings of his loving me. It was incredible, he was incredible ... and the pleasure began to build once again in my core, more and more, with every pass of his cool manipulations.

I writhed when I felt the smooth object slide deep inside me, while I moaned and grasped at his strong forearms in delight. *Yes. This.*

Large and long and firm and slick ... and suddenly I knew. I recognized the sensation of one of my favorite dildos, a beautiful glass piece of art that never failed to hit its mark. My pussy gripped the glass shaft tightly, eager for more, as he penetrated me with slow, rhythmic motions — in and out, in and out, sliding between my slick folds, deeper and deeper. I thought I could not be more aroused, but when he leaned forward to simultaneously lap at my clit, I let out a cry of pure surprise and pleasure. *This man is a magician.*

I could no longer withstand the suspense. I needed release now. My thighs started to twitch as he redoubled his efforts to bring me to climax. I grabbed fistfuls of blankets and sheets, my breathing fast and shallow as I arched into the most delicious orgasm that seemed to never end. He held me there, suspended in ecstasy, until slowly he pulled back, his eyes watching me intensely as he kissed the inside of my thigh and told me he loved me.

Trust really was the hottest thing we'd ever brought into the bedroom, and it was a gift that kept on giving.

Chapter 7
DESSERT

He Said...

With her, there was always something fascinating to discover or learn — about her, about us, about myself. We had just spent a day running errands, holding hands at shopping centers and making small-talk with employees at the post office. We giggled together about the enthusiastic department store clerk who waved and shouted "thank you for your business!" when we were nearly out the door. Then we somehow found ourselves in a heated debate about the pros and cons of buying versus leasing a car (ever the business student, she can't help but go deep on conversations that involve the concepts of depreciation, opportunity cost, or compounding interest).

Finally, we stopped off for a leisurely lunch. Sitting at a booth next to a window, we could both feel the mood shifting as our "to do" list got shorter and we got closer and closer to having earned some quiet time at home, in bed. The mid-day sun was streaming into the restaurant and making it hard to see. She put on her sunglasses and took a sip of her drink through a straw. "I love your lips," I said, transfixed in this simple moment. "Then you should kiss them for hours on end," she said. "Like a good, old-fashioned make-out session. You know, pretend I'm not a sure thing and that you actually have to work for it." I laughed.

Not long after lunch, we arrived back at my place, tossed our retail treasures on the kitchen counter and headed to the bedroom, where we collapsed on top of the comforter and started rearranging the pillows. Lying side by side, fully clothed, we began kissing, caressing, whispering. She had mentioned during lunch that we had never really "made out" … at least not since we'd left our teenage years in the rearview mirror. She was right. And I, of course, was eager to accommodate. Our deep, exploring kisses elicited sighs and quiet moans, our bodies leaned into each other's caresses. I pulled my body up and swung a leg over her middle, as I lowered my lips to her neck. Soft, barely perceptible kisses on her neck drew her hands under the back of my shirt in response. Soft hands caressed my lower back, sparking a strong need to grind against her in my jeans like I was still a teenager. But unlike the awkward unknowns of youthful desire, I think we were both fairly certain where this make-out session would end up. Urgency increasing, I knelt upright, placing both warm palms under her shirt, against her belly. Drawing my hands up slowly, I exposed her pale, silken flesh. As I slid my body down her legs, denim upon denim, I licked a circle around her navel as my hands continued their journey upward. My heart raced as my fingertips found the bottom edge of her lacy bra.

In a flourish of magical movements only a woman can master, my love removed her top, presenting to me the view she knew I was craving. (*My god, she always has the best lingerie*). As I kissed and licked up her body, my hands reached up to pull the bra straps from her freckled shoulders. I couldn't help but think that a cock needed to be shoved between those breasts. Grinning, I helped her remove the sexy bra, exposing her perfect tits, each tipped with a perfectly pink areola and small, pert nipple. My knees astride her hips, I lowered my watering mouth to her chest. I licked along the flesh, moving ever closer to her sensitive tips, pausing to run my tongue around the pebbled surface where her pale skin met the blush of her nipples. I took her into my mouth, sucking deeply, creating suction as I swirled my tongue around the hardened bud. Her hands played with my hair as she drew me tighter to her chest. "Oh, fuck … yes. Just like that," she breathed.

Hmm, I've got a fun idea. I raised my body, trapping her nipple in my mouth, testing the weight of her breast as it lifted from her chest. I glanced up briefly, smiling as I saw her eyes clenched shut, her lower lip trapped between her teeth. I abruptly released her nipple, letting her breast drop back in wave of flesh, undulating beautifully. I attacked the other side, licking my lips and placing them around the sensitive tip. Moving my head slowly, then faster side to side, I let her nipple slide between my slick lips, before capturing it, gently, between my teeth. With the barest of pressure, I tugged it and released, tugged and released. "You need to be in me. Right. Fucking. Now." *Heh, she's so demanding.* And I loved it when she was.

We hurriedly removed our clothing, articles flying about the room. I chuckled to myself as I felt my need growing rapidly, like I was again that overexcited teenage boy, and worried that this was not going to be my best performance. Her body, her scent, the caresses, kisses, and, my god, her insistent demands had me balanced on a knife's edge of control. I quickly knelt between her creamy thighs, gazing for a moment in wonder at the wispy strawberry-blonde hair that framed the glistening folds of her pussy. My left arm wrapped around her leg, as I grabbed my cock in my right hand, hard and nearly bursting. I rubbed the sensitive underside (*oh god, too sensitive*) against her erect clit, before reversing course and slowly, with great concentration and (I thought) heroic deliberation, pushed the head into the confines of her hot, wet sex. Almost immediately, I felt the exhilarating (disappointing?) rush of impending release. I tried every mind trick I knew to stave off the inevitable, including praying to various deities (*Priapis, are you there?*) to no avail. As I sunk deeply into her, my balls constricted and every fiber of my being succumbed to the hormonal wildfire. "Oh ffffuuuuccccckkk!" My back arched, my body tensed, and my head shot back in ecstasy. I drained every ounce of my cum into her body, each pulse eagerly feeding her hungry passage. I attempted to carry on, knowing that she couldn't have possibly reached her own climax in my unexpected rush. I delivered a few feeble thrusts with my spent dick until the intense sensitivity became too much to bear. Sated, yet self-conscious about the premature end to our lovemaking, I pulled out, my copious seed flowing from within to coat her pussy in our combined juices.

"No, not yet ..." She pouted.

"I'm so sorry," I gave her a lopsided smirk. "I can't help it if you're too damned sexy!"

She winked and smiled, "Well I don't need you inside me to cum ..."

Admittedly, I was initially taken aback thinking about my cum already dripping out of her pussy. But that soon gave way to acceptance and hunger as I sunk between her thighs, admiring the sight of my cum, mingled with her juices before me. I lunged forward and with one long lick up the length of her slit, taking our combined spend into my mouth. *Hmm. The salty must be me, 'cause the sweet sure as fuck is her.* I lapped at her pussy, cleaning away all traces of our lovemaking.

"That is so fucking hot!" she moaned. Sucking her pink, inner lips into my mouth, I sought out every drop, exploring deeper and deeper, reaching as far as my tongue would allow, drawing it through every crease and fold. Finally satisfied that I had accomplished my goal, I moved to attack her throbbing, erect clit. "Fuck yes! I'm going to cum in your mouth." *Yeah. You are.*

I sucked her clit hard, pushing her hood back and licking circles around the sensitive bud. I flicked it with the tip of my tongue, lapping as if I was dying of thirst and she was my salvation. With my free hand, I curled my fingers into her warm passage, palm up, seeking the pebbly, textured patch of her G-spot. Successful, I hooked my hand around her pubic bone and began pulling and rubbing furiously at that elusive, magic spot. I placed my mouth fully over her clit, sucking at the sensitive button as I shook my head rapidly, side to side. I began humming against her, the vibrations adding to her pleasure. Her gasps and moans gave way to more guttural, primal grunts and cries. Suddenly I could hear nothing as her entire body tensed, trapping me between her clenching thighs, her hands pressing my face to her sex. She let a long, high wail escape as she thrashed through an intense climax. Finally, her body released, followed by a seemingly endless tide of aftershocks that I held and caressed her through. Her body trembled beneath me, her voice caught and hitched.

"Oh my god, thank you! No one has ever ... wow ..."

No, my lady. Thank you! (An important lesson in sexual etiquette — you are never satisfied properly until your love is properly satisfied.)

I closed my eyes and laughed.

"What?" she asked.

"Nothing," I said. "I was just thinking about that guy at the store who shouted 'thank you for your business!'"

She laughed so hard she could barely catch her breath. Then she sat up very straight, wiped the smile off her face, and pantomimed a big farewell wave while whispering, "No, thank you for *your* business!"

My god, I adored that silly, sexy, incorrigible, impossibly perfect woman.

She Said ...

For some people, Sundays are for worship or for rest. For me, they're usually about catching up on what didn't get finished during the week. They're for errands and "to do" lists, household chores and bills to pay. And sometimes, they're for a kind of worship that happens in the bedroom.

That Sunday, my "to do" list was long and my motivation was running short, so I called him and said, "Errands are boring. Come with me." I picked him up a few minutes later and handed him the scribbled list. "Where are we going first?" he asked.

First up was the post office. He made a joke about the "impressive package" in the back seat of my car, to which I retorted, "That's what she said." And I watched him inside the post office, chatting up the clerks and instantly holding in awe the 20-something girl in line behind us and the 50-something woman behind the counter. Women everywhere were captivated by him. I rarely felt jealous; it actually made me feel a tiny bit powerful and proud, knowing that none of his adoring fans knew him intimately, as I did.

Eventually, after stopping by a few different stores and scratching everything off the list of errands that I had penned that morning, we both admitted we had nothing of interest in the pantry or refrigerator at home, so we stopped off at a casual restaurant for some lunch. It was sunny and bright, and while it was cold outside, our booth by the window was warm. I took off my jacket and basked in it for a moment. He sometimes gets quiet when his mind is wandering, and while he'd been chatty all day, he was quiet as we were finishing our meals. "Whatcha thinkin'?" I asked. "Oh, so many things," he said and smiled. I shook my head. I could tell we were already at home in bed, as far as he was concerned. Better get him out of this diner before his jeans are too tight or he reaches under the table to caress more than just my kneecap.

So we headed back to his place, and to the bedroom.

What I love about our lovemaking? All of it. The silly moments and the hot moments. The long sessions and the quickies. The surprises and the classics. Even the moments when it seems we might disappoint one another — because it's in those moments we usually rise to the challenge in toe-tingling ways.

I loved kissing his perfect mouth and soft lips. I loved that he often tasted like mints or cinnamon candy. Of course he really had the perfect *everything*, which meant I often got ahead of myself when we were together. I never lingered long enough over our kisses because I would be eagerly fumbling with his belt. I never melted sufficiently into his hugs because I was already slipping my hands up inside his shirt.

So I decided to keep my focus this time. "You know, we never really make out ... like we did when we were teenagers ..." It was something I had mentioned perhaps 30 minutes ago at the restaurant, and I was still thinking about it so I said it again.

"Mmm ..." he replied and leaned in for a kiss. And another. And another. It was delicious. Closing our eyes and getting lost in one another, in no hurry to get to another position or the next orgasm. But change position he did. He rose up off his hip, where he had been nestled next to me on top of the covers, and rolled me gently back so my shoulders rested on the pillows. In a swift, graceful movement, I found him straddling me and leaning down into a deeper kiss. I could feel him, swollen and warm, through his jeans as I wrapped my legs around his hips. Even after all these years, I felt a sort of sexy pride at being able to elicit such strong responses from his body with "just" a kiss. I reached up for him, tangling my fingers in his hair, moaning. I don't know if we'd been kissing for a minute or an hour, but it was so incredibly hot. I felt closer to him in this moment than ever before. I loved when he humored my ideas in the bedroom. (*Goodness knows, I humored his, too. And loved every minute.*)

With us, of course, it was never just a kiss. And fortunately we were no longer awkward teenagers, so we both knew fourth base was a sure thing. He slipped his hand under my shirt, taking breaks from kissing my face to kiss my belly button and to remove one item of clothing at a time.

I slipped out of my lacy bra, tossing it halfway across the room, and the kisses kept coming. Across my shoulders, between and along the curves of my breasts, his mouth pausing to suck one nipple and then the other. *Our teenage kissing was* nothing *like this. But I like that he's revising history as we go!*

I kept rising up to nibble his neck and moan sweet-nothings into his ears while he played a sort of ping-pong with my breasts, lifting them gently with his teeth, one at a time, and kissing me here, there, and everywhere.

I was loving every bit of it. But my body was impatient. My internal fire was burning hot and I needed him. Inside me. Now.

And I told him so.

He sighed in that "I pretend to hate how impatient you are" way. But the look on his face said it all. There's nothing more satisfying than knowing your lover can't go another second without you.

We started tearing off the rest of our clothes — clearly done with our "make-out session" for the time being — and throwing them haphazardly about the room. I heard something hit a lamp shade and laughed.

He wrinkled his nose and raised an eyebrow as if to say, "You ready for this?" I nodded and he deftly pulled my thighs open and guided his smooth, hard cock into me. I could actually hear the slick sound of him sliding into place. *My god, we're so hot together.*

The first thrust took my breath away. It nearly always did, as if my body and my heart were still surprised by how good it felt to be filled up, by how amazing it was to be his. And then we were lost in the moment, slipping and grinding, so incredibly wet and needy. I felt him stiffen further inside me as the muscles in his forearms went ropy and tense and his back arched suddenly as he climaxed, hard, groaning and biting his bottom lip.

I love it when he surrenders. I love what I do to him.

He continued to thrust until he was clearly spent, and collapsed onto the bed next to me. But I was all amped up and craving my own release. *It's only fair, right?*

"No … Not yet …" I said, kissing him gently and wiggling around on the pillows as if I might throw a sex-goddess tantrum if I didn't get an orgasm too.

Never one to keep a sex-goddess waiting, he got back to his knees and bent down to lick and taste me. To lick and taste *us* — his cum mingling with my own wet arousal — tentatively at first, then with vigor. His tongue like silk against the slickness of my pussy, tickling and titillating. He gripped the insides of my thighs and settled into a rhythm. *Oh my god … it was so good.*

"This is so fucking hot," I gasped. Or maybe I just thought it. I can't be sure.

The nerve endings in my clit were dancing with pleasure as he sucked and flicked it with his tongue, sliding a finger, then two, inside me. I was never going to last. Like his, my body was especially eager today, wanting to rush to the finish line, hungry for satisfaction. So I let go, felt my hips sink deeper into the comforter, my back arching as the orgasm rose up in my pelvis like a wave just before it furiously explodes over the edge of a pier. My throat caught as I called out his name, again and again, hoping he enjoyed this sweet dessert as much as I did.

Chapter 8
STRAWBERRIES AND BRIE

He Said...

Our encounters are never dull, never monotonous or routine. Sometimes they are rushed and frenetic, but equally, they can be lingering and relaxed. On some occasions, they combine the best of both worlds. Those are the times when our passions can't be contained and we cannot be denied our carnal desires, but also when we can be vulnerable, romantic, and our lovemaking slow, relaxed, and intense.

Such was the case on one rainy-day rendezvous. I walked down the hall to the door, my heart hammering in my chest in anticipation of our first kiss. I hadn't seen her in weeks, as life had gotten in the way and a litany of work commitments, projects around the house, and kids' sports matches had filled my schedule to the point that, try as I might, I had been unable to sneak out even for a few hours for what I craved the most. A few hours of her, in my arms. But even when we hadn't been absent for any period of time, it was always like this; every meeting with her held the excitement of a first date. I knocked quietly, knowing she'd be expecting me. It quickly opened as if she'd been waiting just as excitedly on the other side. *Mmm, perfect, as usual.* She greeted me with a gentle, chaste kiss, and took my coat as I shut the door behind me. I slipped in for another kiss. I do love her kisses.

She smiled at me with the glee of a child and pulled at my hand. "Come see!" She practically skipped into the room to unveil the surprise. *Oh. My. God. A Jacuzzi for two.* "Oh, we'll be using that," I said softly, smiling at her happiness. The combination of her youthful enthusiasm, the lure of promised delights in the Jacuzzi, and just her presence, had a profound effect on me. I wrapped her in my arms, walking her backward as I covered her lips with mine. I was mindless of our destination, until a soft, "Oh ..." told me we'd found the cool backdrop of a window pane. The soft trickling of rain against the window accompanied her light sighs and moans as I pressed against her body. Kisses rained down as hands traveled and explored. Instinctively, I pressed my hardness into her, wanting her to feel how excited I was. My hands explored her body, exposing her breasts as my thumbs rubbed over her sensitive, erect nipples. She placed her own hands on either side of my face as if to hold my kisses in place, before she slipped one hand behind my head and the other travelled down my body to release my straining cock from the confines of my jeans.

Suddenly, the tables had turned. Now she was driving me blindly backward until the backs of my knees met the edge of the bed. With a gentle push, I sat down on the comforter, looking up at my lovely goddess, breasts bare, nipples pink and hard. "Time to get naked," she said, removing my shirt, pants, and, teasingly slowly, my boxers. As my cock came into view, she grinned wickedly, giving me a slow lick, base to tip, causing pre-cum to pool and slowly drip from its head. She stood to remove her pants and panties, pausing to give me that, "I'm going to devour you" look that drives me crazy. *Not this time, lady,* I thought to myself, as I reached up and pulled her onto the bed with me. Somehow (I like to believe it was graceful) I maneuvered her to her back with her head on a pillow, as I straddled her legs. My eyes roamed over the delectable treat before me. I leaned forward and moved my attentions down her body, kissing her fully upon the lips, lightly upon each nipple, teasingly on her tummy, and finishing hungrily on her sex.

Oh, how I adored her pussy. So pink, wet, and delicious, with light tufts of strawberry-blonde hair, framing perfectly shaped lips, currently glistening with her own dew. As I admired her perfection, she slowly spread those lips open for me, two fingers pulling her labia apart, inviting me to partake in a taste. "Mmm," I moaned as I dipped my tongue between the folds, tasting the tangy sweetness of her body.

"Mmm, yes baby, like that."

"Right there, don't stop."

"Ooh, fuck yes, yes."

As I tongue-fucked her pussy and sucked her hard clit, I heard the hottest words ever uttered in the throes of passion: "I'm going to come in your fucking mouth." *Oh, yes. Yes, you are. Guaranteed.*

With that ultimate encouragement, I slipped one, then a second finger into her, seeking out the magical G-spot. While probing and caressing that rough, pebbly surface, I sucked her clit in between my lips and lashed it quickly with my tongue. The rhythmic thrusts in and out of her gloriously wet sex, along with my persistent attentions at her clit, finally provided her release as she came hard in my mouth, flooding it with her warm, sweet, fluids. As she rode through her climax — thighs clenching, tummy trembling, voice shaking, back arched, and hands gripping the sheets tightly — I raised myself to my knees, grabbed her upper thighs and pushed myself into her deeply in one thrust. Her eyes opened wide in surprise and lust as I began urgently bucking my hips. I intended to have her reach her next climax in time with my own.

She thrashed about, mindless in her pleasure, as her hands grasped at me in seeming desperation. Her tight velvet sex gripped my cock hungrily as I drove into her harder and faster. I felt the pressure welling up in my body. The clenching began at my toes and surged up my legs, the muscles and nerves of my body firing haphazardly, urging me into a frenzy. I could hear the slapping sounds of our bodies as the wetness of our arousal smacked with every thrust. I could sense her body growing closer and closer to falling over the edge. Urgent words of encouragement and need filled the air. Finally, with one last fierce thrust, I emptied every ounce of myself into her as her body clenched and throbbed out her own release. Our eyes opened wide as we stared lovingly at each other. Collapsing to the bed, I pulled her close and held her tight as aftershocks rocked her body in a way that made her feel at once vulnerable and fierce, beautiful and all mine.

We lay together for a moment as we recovered, cuddling and loving each other. "I have another surprise," she said as she sat up and crawled off the bed. Tiptoeing over to a table in the corner, she uncovered a plate full of strawberries and cheese. Leave it to this lady to bring a spread of delicacies straight out of one of her Victorian romance novels. As we drew water for the Jacuzzi, watching it fill, we lazily enjoyed the juxtaposition of the sweet berries and the soft, savory cheese, Once the steamy water had filled the tub, we grabbed the plate and some fresh bottles of chilled water, and slipped in for a leisurely soak. We talked a while and laughed, absently stroking each other's bare skin under the heat of the churning water. Soon, however, those absent-minded touches became more deliberate, more insistent. Her delicate little fingers slid up my inner thigh, stopping to cup my balls, and massage the sensitive area underneath.

"Back to bed?" she asked, one eyebrow lifting mischievously.

"Oh yes, yes indeed."

Hastily, we dried ourselves, unconcerned about getting the bed a little wet. She pushed me down onto the bed and sensually drew her damp body along mine, tracing licks and kisses down my form. My cock jumped to attention as she licked and swirled her tongue around its tip before taking me deeply into her warm, inviting mouth. She had this technique that, if I was standing, would have buckled my knees. She slid her tongue up and down the underside of my stiff rod, around the head, then pulled away, teasing. She moved to straddle my legs and lowered herself deliciously, inch by inch, onto my engorged member. She leaned down to kiss me while stroking me with her slippery pussy. Every part of my body locked momentarily as a torrent of cum burst forth, filling her channel. But I was not done with her yet. I could hear our bodies smacking together as she continued to work my tumescent penis.

I felt empowered as my cock stayed hard and ready. I had a sense of invincibility. I flipped her onto her back and smoothly reentered the warm silkiness of her sex. I drove into her with purpose, hard and deep, seeking our mutual pleasure. I heard her breath coming in shorter and shorter gasps and knew her climax was imminent. I slowed. *I can be a tease, too,* I smiled. I shifted her body so that she was laying on her side while I straddled her thigh, expertly maneuvering our bodies around each other without separating from the warm clutch of her sex on my cock.

"Oh, my. So deep, I like this," she moaned.

"Let's call it a new twist on an old classic."

The position allowed me to enter her more thoroughly, more deeply. It provided just the right angle to stimulate her G-spot as we gyrated and thrust against one another, until together we felt the tingling of another imminent release. I bent to kiss her lips just as we came in perfect unison. It was a powerful moment — her achieving an orgasm from penetration, us climaxing together, the marvelous surprise of a long-lasting erection, a day full of delight after delight.

Ultimately satiated, we collapsed into a heap of warm, glistening body parts, kisses that tasted like strawberries, and a peaceful, loving sleep ... a rest that cemented another memory of amazing lovemaking into our minds.

She Said ...

Rainy days had always been lucky for us, so I didn't let it spoil my mood when I woke up to gray clouds and cold raindrops outside my windows. Our romantic morning getaway was going to be beautiful. It had been several weeks since I'd seen him, and I surely wasn't going to let the weather get in the way.

When he finally knocked on the door, I scampered over to let him in with a shy "Hi ..." before kissing him softly and taking his coat. Every hello for us still felt like the beginning of a first date — full of nerves and possibility. I always wanted to be perfect for him in every way because he was always everything I was hoping for. The second he entered a room, I suddenly felt safe, calm, peaceful, loved. I think he could feel it too.

"Mmmm ..." He stole another kiss.

"Come see!" I grabbed his hand and took him through our suite into the bedroom. I pointed excitedly: *A hot tub built for two!*

His eyes lit up and he raised one eyebrow coyly. "We'll be using that."

Yes, yes, we would.

And without another word, my shoulders were pressed against the window panes as the rain pelted at the glass behind me. He explored my mouth with fervent, delicious kisses while he unbuttoned my blouse and let it fall to the floor. My bare shoulders pressed against the cool glass, his warm hands discarding my bra and cupping my breasts. I ran a hand through his soft hair, while the temptation of his hard cock pressing against me drew my other hand down to unbutton his jeans.

"Pretend you're pressed between two panes of glass," my yoga instructor once said, trying to get me into the perfect pose. Had she thought to say "pretend you're pressed between a pane of glass and the throbbing cock of the man you love …" she might have been more successful in getting me into form. *Holy hell, he was amazing!* Every touch, every murmur, every confident move. I was ready to orgasm and I hadn't even parted with all my clothes yet!

Hungry for more, I pushed him backward until he fell into a sitting position on the side of the bed. "You're not naked enough," I told him, then proceeded to remove every stitch of clothing from his body. I shimmied myself out of my own jeans and panties, and paused for just a moment to admire us. Him, with his biceps flexed as he braced on the edge of the bed, his cock standing at attention and glistening with pre-cum. Me, standing just inches from him, nipples hard, thighs flushed with anticipation.

He reached for my hand and pulled me onto the bed to join him. He adjusted the pillow beneath my head before sliding possessively down my body, leaving a trail of kisses as he went. He put amateurs to shame with his methods of foreplay. With his skills, it was more aptly called bliss … nirvana … scream-out-loud pleasure. It was a kind of worship.

I closed my eyes and took a slow breath while reaching one hand down to spread the lips of my pussy for him in an act of invitation and need. I wanted to be his goddess, to be sure he could see me, smell me, taste me more fully.

"Mmmm," he moaned as he dipped his tongue in for the first time, tasting me as one might sample honey from a jar. Seemingly satisfied that I was as sweet as he imagined, he licked again and again, pressing the tip of his nose against my clit in a way that made me wild. I clutched at the bed linens and prayed he'd never stop. He stiffened his tongue, driving it deep into me while rapidly stroking my clit with one finger. I bucked with pleasure. "Yes, just like that ... don't stop ..."

But he was a tease. He pulled back and opened my thighs wide, moving the attentions of his tongue to the delicate skin where my pelvis met my thigh. *Oh.* He slid two fingers inside me, casually and smoothly, as he continued to lick and kiss and suck my thigh. He moved back toward my core, kissing the patch of pubic hair just above where his hand was rhythmically exploring my slick passage, seeking out that sweet spot inside. "Oh, god ..."

He dove back into my sex while his fingers continued their assault, face first, moaning as he licked every bit of me. I reached my hands out and desperately grabbed at anything I could find to keep my body from floating into the air. "Now. Oh, fuck. Right now ... I'm going to come in your mouth ... oh, baby, don't stop ...!!!"

And then I screamed. All-out screamed with delight and surprise and gratitude as every muscle in my body stiffened and trembled and hot juices came flowing out of me and into his hungry, waiting mouth.

Oh. My. God.

I was still trembling when he rose to his knees and slid his cock into me. Hard. I sucked in my breath with surprise.

Again ... I wanted him to do it again.

He looked me in the eyes and rocked his hips slowly from side to side, so we could feel every point of connection. He slid almost all the way out before ramming his length back into me, my slick providing no resistance. "YES!!" My eyes rolled up into my head as I thrust my hips forward, crashing my pelvis into his, over and over.

Is it possible for a man to be harder than hard? He filled me so completely, and we fit together so fucking perfectly. "This. Oh, god ... yes, this," I moaned as I thrashed, not just loving him as I always do, but all-out ravishing him, clutching at his arms and chest, arching up to kiss him wherever I could reach, wanting (needing) to fuck and be fucked until I could no longer think straight. He slowed for just a second, always the gentleman, taking a moment to look me in the eyes to ensure I was feeling safe and happy and comfortable. " … yes …" I whispered. Then I gyrated my hips to pull him deeper into me, feeling his throbbing cock give a final pump as he burst forth, filling my passage with his hot cum. He screamed too.

Entirely exhausted, we eventually managed to gather up our happy hearts and turn our thoughts to our other basic human needs: food and water.

Of course I had come prepared for just such a moment, as I uncovered a plate of fresh, juicy strawberries and a small wheel of brie to complement them. It was the perfect combination of sweet and savory to moisten our tastebuds after our exertions. "Mmmm …" He shook his head and smiled while savoring a bite of sweet fruit — acknowledging his appreciation for my continued dedication to the smallest details. I wouldn't deign to serve him anything less than exquisite after that kind of performance.

I found myself curling up closer and closer against him as my body cooled and a chill came on. "Join me in the Jacuzzi?" I asked.

"Mmmm hmmm."

We were compatible even in this way … both loving a nearly scalding hot bath to soothe our muscles and relax our minds. We slid together into the large, oval tub, our arms and legs lovingly intertwined, our hands roving over each other's body. It was heaven.

In absolutely no hurry to go anywhere or do anything, we pampered ourselves in the hot, bubbling water for an hour, talking about our morning and about favorite memories and even about current events. I'd always loved him for his wit; he was a great conversationalist and a deep thinker. And wickedly funny, sometimes in wry, unexpected ways.

Before long, our roving hands and warm, wet bodies tore down my walls of control. All my thoughts, save one, disappeared. *I needed him.*

I transitioned my soft, gentle caresses — on his hands, knees, calves, forearms — to something a bit more deliberate and sensual. I massaged the insides of his thighs and trailed my fingertips around his balls and applied pressure to the area just below. He sat up straighter in the tub as I teased him.

I looked him in the eyes and kissed him. Firmly. He reciprocated as I could feel his cock jump against my arm as I massaged his perineum. I leaned down to kiss his wet chest where it emerged from the water and sucked at one of his nipples. He sighed softly.

"Wanna go back to bed?" I asked.

"Yes. Yes, I do."

We scrambled out of the tub, barely toweling ourselves dry before tumbling back into bed and crawling under the covers to retain our body heat.

"Lay back and relax," I said, winking and rising to my knees, the blankets draped loosely over my back. It was time for me to give him the blowjob he so deserved. With one hand on the inside of his thigh and the other wrapped around the base of his dick, I lowered my head and took a moment to breathe in the intoxicating scent of his damp, clean skin. I began licking the head of his cock and slowly swirling my tongue around the shaft. I heard his sharp intake of breath over the background of raindrops tap, tap, tapping upon the windows. He was stiffening further. *Oh, god, that was so hot.* I opened my mouth wide to take him inside, sucking quickly on the head before pulling him in deep where I could suck, and taste, and feel him, hard, against my throat. He groaned and closed his eyes.

He was perfectly groomed and an anatomical work of art. Symmetrical and smooth, warm and pink. I once told him he had a "beautiful penis," and he carried that compliment like a badge of honor. I loved admiring it as I went back and forth between teasing him with the tip of my tongue, feeling the soft head of his cock brush against my nose, and sliding him back past my lips to swallow him deep. I was salivating as I tended to him, letting out tiny slurping noises that made me want to giggle with glee. I loved the noises our bodies made together.

Opening my mouth a bit wider, I pistoned his hard member in and out while my hand stroked and gripped him firmly at its base. I could feel the muscles in his body tensing. Unable to deny myself the sensation of him coming inside me, I resisted the urge to bring him to climax and swallow all he was about to offer. Instead, I jumped up to straddle him, settling him inside me while I grabbed his shoulders and kissed him hard. I began riding him in a smooth, elliptical rhythm. While I cried out to him about how good he felt, I heard him moan, "yes, oh god, yes" until his arms shot out to grab me hard. He thrust his cock deep inside me as he orgasmed, filling my pussy with his warm seed, but I could not stop. I kept pumping my body over him, milking his cum with delight.

He was, amazingly, still hard. Like a tireless teenager, he flipped me onto my back and slid back into me, taking over the proverbial driver's seat. I gazed up at him in awe as he smiled and began rotating his hips, first one way, then the next, testing out angles and positions, listening for my responses as our bodies connected here, there, everywhere. I was at the very edge of my own climax when he twisted my body underneath him into a new position that took my breath away. *Wow.* With my ass bumping against his hip, he was able to slide in just a tiny bit deeper ... and that tiny bit made a world of difference.

"This is new ..." I teased as I felt my body reacting hungrily to the new sensation. "I like it. Oh, yeah, wow. I really like it."

He replied in a perfect soundbite that would become a favorite phrase of ours: "It's a new twist on an old classic."

Indeed.

When it comes to lovemaking, there is usually a moment when you know it's coming to an end — to a fevered climax, a slowing down and a sort of sensual denouement. But this day was different. Our bodies were tireless. The more we felt, the more we wanted. Perhaps the berries were an aphrodisiac, or perhaps the sex gods were looking down upon us — all I know is that this moment, this day, was epic. As his cock reached into my greatest depths, rubbing along the mysterious G-spot, tears of ecstasy filled the corners of my eyes. My mind was rapt at the novelty of what was about to happen ... *I can't believe it. I'm going to come during intercourse ... he's not even touching my clit.* I love intercourse — always had — but nearly always needed clitoral stimulation to reach climax. But not today.

I was clutching his limbs like a starving woman as he pounded into me, again and again. He was moaning. I was moaning. "Kiss me," I gasped.

And as he bent over our hot, sweaty, twisted bodies and slid his tongue into my mouth, my body let go. I could feel my sex clenching onto his cock as it spasmed. So tight, so uncontrolled, so beautifully raw.

"I love you," he whispered.

"I can't believe ..." I attempted and then stopped. He couldn't believe it either. Orgasm after orgasm, our bodies rose to the challenge. He had never been more handsome or strong in my eyes. So vulnerable and yet so in control. So fearless and yet so loving. He tucked a lock of my hair behind my ear as I swallowed hard, thirsty and unable to keep my eyes off of him. His steely blue eyes stared back into mine, conveying so much in that moment, telling stories about where we'd been, where we were headed, and why no person or circumstance could ever break this connection we shared. We made love until we dropped from exhaustion, then snuggled beneath a tangle of sheets and blankets as we drifted off to a place where even the dreams could not rival our reality.

Chapter 9
BLACK RIBBONS

He Said ...

Variety and surprise are the spices that make life so delicious, particularly with a woman who provides plenty of both. I had an idea for variety and spice myself on this particular day.

I had just finished brushing my teeth and combing my hair when I heard her enter the bedroom.

"Be right out, make yourself at home," I called out, checking myself in the mirror one last time. Exiting the bathroom, I walked toward her in what I hoped was a confident manner, despite the butterflies that seemed to always appear in my stomach when we met. One must have fluttered up to my heart this time, because it skipped a beat as I drew close enough to smell her delicate perfume.

"Beautiful," I said as I placed teasing kisses along her lower lip, wanting to draw out her seeking tongue. As if on cue, I felt a tentative flick against my lips. Obligingly, I parted them to savor the first intimate contact of her tongue on mine. Never lose your love of kissing. There's so much love and trust transferred in the simple, yet emotionally complex connection. It never fails to arouse me either, which is a nice side effect.

Leaning back ever so slightly, she looked down between us, noticing the effect she was having on me. She slowly stroked the palm of her hand along my length, rigid underneath the workout shorts I was wearing.

"I like," she whispered. "Mmm, I need," she followed with a squeeze.

In my excitement, I moved to grasp the bottom of her shirt and pull it off, but she caught me by surprise and swiftly bent down to remove my shorts in one fluid motion. I gasped as I felt her face make contact with the head of my freed cock. As she stood, I removed my shirt, eager to feel her bare flesh on mine as soon as possible. But she surprised me again as she turned and crawled onto the bed, sashaying her scrumptious (though still fully clothed) ass in front of me in a way that had me harder than hard.

I stepped over to meet her at the bed just as she turned her body to face mine, my hungry cock waving in her face. She parted her lips through a smile as I drew myself up a little taller, placing her at just the right height to slide her tongue along my shaft. As if finally realizing we were both wearing too many clothes, she abruptly sat upright, arms shooting over her head in an invitation. The remainder of our clothes were flung to the corners of the room before I eagerly helped her to a comfortable position on her back. Out of the corner of my eye, I spied two silky, black ribbons lying next to her on the mattress. I hadn't removed any ribbons from her clothing, so I was curious about where they had come from ... and what they were for.

"What are these?" I asked, handing her the thin strips of material. She took one and slipped it over her wrist, the purpose suddenly becoming clear, "In case you'd like to tie up my wrists ... or ankles ... or both ..." She smiled mischievously as her eyes became dreamy and distant for a moment. I wondered what she was thinking.

"A little light bondage, eh, sweetie?" I laughed while gently parting her knees. She was already so wet, the pink lips of her pussy glistened in the light streaming in from the window. I smiled and stroked my fingers gently through her folds. I looked deeply into her eyes as I brought those fingers to my lips, sucking the dew of her sweet essence into my mouth.

I sat up on my knees, still smiling. "Roll over, baby," I ordered. She surprised me with a cheeky "Yes, sir!" as she slowly, sensually rotated her body underneath me. I raised my body over hers, my cock bumping against her, teasingly — *not yet, baby*. I bent down to kiss her lower back, running my tongue near that taboo area of my desire. Slowly and deliberately, I dipped my tongue into the cleavage of her perfect, round ass. I licked slow, sliding deeper with every pass, up to the dimple of her lower back and returning, deeper still. I placed my hands upon her smooth cheeks, kneading, squeezing, parting, as I slipped ever lower.

I had a destination in mind but was damn determined to enjoy the journey. My next pass finally brought me in contact with her tight little rosebud. She gasped as the moisture of my tongue cooled the sensitive skin. Her body bucked a bit under the sensation, and then she moaned throatily as she settled in, surrendering to the pleasure. I let go of one of her cheeks, sliding my finger from the edge of her tight hole, down, and alongside (but not in) her dripping pussy. With a momentary thought to safety, I shifted my weight just enough to reach the bedside table, where I opened the drawer and grabbed a wet wipe. I deftly wiped my fingers, tossing the towelette back on the table and resuming my exploration.

I sought out her sensitive clit with my fingers, determined to fill her body with as much sensation and pleasure as possible. Another audible gasp, followed by, "Oh fuck yes, fuck me harder, harder," drove me into an incredible lust. I teased, stroked, and circled her clit harder and faster. My tongue danced across her pucker, tickling, flicking, stroking flat tongued, and probing as deep as I could. Her back arched and she pushed her ass back into me. I could sense her impending climax before she began to plead with hungry desire, urging me to finish her, finish her now. Her orgasm was explosive, forcing her lower body even harder into mine, demanding to be touched in every intimate way. With a shout, she collapsed fully, twitching with aftershocks, over and over.

I held her gently, gazing upon her satiated body in the pale moonlight. Finally, she turned to me with a smirk, "Your turn." *Oh, yeah.*

"Mmm ... Be right back," I mumbled, padding barefoot to the bathroom to rinse my mouth, have a drink of water and clean up a bit.

I crawled back into bed alongside her, feeling safe and satisfied to be touching her again after a momentary separation. I settled into the pillows with my arms around her and said, "So … you said something about *my* turn?" Without the slightest delay, she climbed to her knees, alongside my reclining body. She picked up the satin ribbons and playfully drew them around my smoothly groomed cock and balls. I watched a moment, wondering what it would feel like if she tied that ribbon around the base of my shaft as she sucked me deep into her mouth. I shook myself out of my reverie as her petite hands first cupped my balls and grasped me at the base. *Oh good lord*, she took me to the hilt in one movement, no pretense of teasing, just a carnal need to touch me. She stroked and sucked, bobbing her head slowly, then more swiftly. She knew I was close to losing control when she paused and looked me straight in the eyes, "Please?" Accepting my imploring look as encouragement, she laid back on the bed and pulled me over and into her.

She Said …

He was out of sight in the bathroom when I arrived. "Go ahead and make yourself comfortable. I'll be right there," he called out. I quickly took today's surprise out of my purse and tossed it on the bed. Two satin ribbons, black and delicate-looking against the white comforter. I smiled deviously and took my hair down, anxious to see my man.

"Come here, beautiful," he said, emerging from the bathroom to cradle my face in his hands. He took a deep breath as if committing my smell to memory, and kissed me, softly and slowly. He was warm, his skin still damp from the shower. I teased his lips open with my tongue, inviting myself in, exploring the heat and warmth of him that I knew so well.

He wasn't wearing much, really. Just a t-shirt and a pair of gym shorts, and there was no hiding the growing hardness of his cock underneath. I wasn't about to ignore it. I dropped my hands to grope him through the thin fabric of his shorts. "I like," I breathed.

"I need," I promised.

He always managed to get me naked first, so I was on a mission today to strip him in record time. Giving him no question about where I was headed, I skipped the t-shirt and shimmied his shorts down his muscled thighs and into a puddle of fabric on the floor. *Hmmm, no boxers.* I knelt at his knees and ran the side of my nose along the tip of his cock. His breath caught as he pulled off his t-shirt, anxious to feel nothing between us.

The sun was setting and the room had been cast in a warm shade of gold, making his already tanned skin look positively sun-kissed. His pale eyes sparkled as they seemed to drink me down. I crawled onto the bed, fully clothed, shaking my ass in a way that was sure to drive him insane. He eagerly joined me on the mattress and began stripping me nude.

He paused. "What are these?" He held up the smooth, black strips of satin that I had mischievously placed on the bed earlier.

"In case you want to tie my wrists. Or my ankles. Or both." I grabbed one and slid it over my wrist. *Damn. The visual alone was erotic as hell.* I looked down at the dark ribbon trailing over my pale skin onto the white comforter, the shock of black decidedly naughty in contrast to the sweet, sunset romance surrounding us.

"A little bondage for my sweetheart, eh?" He laughed and drew my legs apart, stroking my pussy with one finger, then two. I was dripping. "Mmmm ..." he moaned and then was lost inside me, his face no longer visible as I ran my fingers through his hair and started to arch with delight as I felt his tongue, lips, nose, fingers absolutely worshipping my every private curve.

"Oh my god," I gasped, letting my hands slide down his strong neck to his shoulders. He flicked my clit with the tip of his tongue as if to say, "Don't worry ... I'm not leaving ..." before rising, pulling me into a sitting position and asking me to get on my knees.

"Yes, sir." I glanced over my shoulder and gave him my best, innocent little smile. I crawled forward to give him plenty of room behind me. He kissed my lower back and took my ass cheeks firmly into his palms. He groaned. I imagined his cock hardening further as his ultimate fantasy played out again. He was so very good at enjoying every detail, and of delaying his final release until after he'd had an eyeful, mouthful, handful, and earful of my body and its pleasure.

He licked a trail from my lower back into that forbidden divide. I shivered and relaxed into the moment. I settled onto my elbows, pitching my ass up toward him at the perfect angle. He reached under me to find my clit with his fingertips, distracting me as he licked and stroked my ass. We were both in heaven.

"Oh, god, yes. Fuck me harder." I cried, my legs and arms beginning to go weak beneath me. "I can't …"

I can't stop myself. I couldn't stop myself from surrendering to the overwhelming sensations. My ears started to buzz and I closed my eyes after catching one final glimpse of my left hand clutching the bed linens, the black ribbons trailing toward my elbow, before everything shattered so beautifully.

He fell onto his side next to me and drew me close, kissing me. The sun was gone and the room was dark but for the pale glow of the moon outside. He was so handsome and so strong. I felt so safe lying there beside him. I always had and I always would.

I snuggled against his side, drawing the sheets over us. When my breathing returned to normal, and after he made a subtle detour to the bathroom to clean up (safety first!) after our foray into ass-play, I was feeling strong and eager. My trembling muscles and racing heart were recovering, so I pulled myself up again to my knees.

"Your turn," I said, sliding the sheets back to uncover the shaft of his perfect cock waiting for me. I dragged the silky ribbons over his chest and thighs, caressing him as I moved toward his manhood, taking him into my mouth. Just the tip at first, swirling my tongue across the velvety expanse and then down around the ridge.

He put one hand around the base of his cock, which I covered with my own fingers and kissed each time my mouth slid downward toward our tangle of hands. I liked to tease him. I sucked him hard and then backed off, inviting him in shallowly, then deeply, when he least expected it. I wanted him to feel every sensation — lips, tongue, teeth, hands, even the cascade of my hair, which fell over my shoulders and tickled his skin. I knew this was one of the million reasons he loved my long hair. "It's part of the sensory experience," he'd told me.

I was so focused on enjoying every curve of him and every moan, that I barely noticed when my own legs began to tremble with excitement and fatigue. *It was time.*

I rolled over onto my back and pulled him on top of me, aligning his dripping member with my expectant pussy. "Please ..." I said sweetly and desperately. He slid inside me, deep and slow and deliberately as I wrapped my arms around his ribcage and my legs around his hips, realizing that, as sexy as the ribbons had been, there was clearly no need to be tied up. He'd already captured me, in every single way.

Chapter 10
MIND-BLOWING

He Said...

She's so cute when she's flouncy. That balance between the physical exuberance and her bubbly personality strikes me as the sexiest mix. That day, her spirit set the tone for everything that followed. When I opened the door, she smiled as she walked into the chaos of barking dogs. Undeterred, she gave the necessary greetings to quell my pups' excitement, then greeted me with a bright, "Hi!" She was already glancing up the stairs, and I had to smile. She was wasting no time tonight.

"After you," I said and followed her as she bounded up the steps, kicking off her shoes as she went. At the top, she spun to face me. I caught her jaw in my hand, holding her still for a moment, and leaned in to kiss her.

I believe certain kisses need to feel like a prelude to lovemaking. A chaste nibble followed by more insistent pressure, finishing with a deep dive and the dancing of intertwined tongues. When hands are introduced to the mix, you have a recipe for knee-buckling intimacy. As I caressed her jawline with one hand, my other reached around to trace the hollow of her back, just above the lace edge of her panties. The curves of her ass beckoned to me as I trailed my fingers lower, backing her awkwardly into the bedroom as I continued exploring her mouth. I was suddenly overcome with need, and I found myself fumbling with the button of her jeans. She gave me a hand as we smiled into our kiss. From beneath half-lidded eyes, she spied my newly acquired Himalayan salt lamp on the bedside table. "Mood lighting?" she asked, smiling against my lips, as her pants dropped unceremoniously to the floor.

"Yeah, I'm romantic like that."

She didn't argue the point.

We continued to undress as articles of clothing were haphazardly abandoned on our way to the bed. I lifted the covers, allowing her to tuck herself into its warmth. I crawled in beside her, resting on my hip and elbow, taking a moment to admire her beauty. Maybe I'm biased, but I swear she doesn't age. She's as stunning now as she was when we were teenagers.

We joined in another long kiss, my hand finding the inside of her thigh, as one of hers teasingly tweaked my nipple. I slowly drew my hand along her smooth skin, ever higher until I felt the soft fluff of her sex and the heat emanating from within. Her legs parted in invitation. The first touch of her moist, pink folds filled me with excitement, combined with the nervous thrill of being involved in something both secretive and new. No one in my world knew about our relationship; yet, in this moment, she *was* my entire world.

As my fingers brushed across her lower lips, I felt the slick of her growing arousal. I turned my hand, palm down, and slid a finger into her silky core — stroking up, down, backward, forward. I smiled as I felt her small hand wrap around my cock. Shocks of desire surged through me. Overwhelmed by the sensation of my hands on her sex, she soon gave up her attempts to reward me, but I didn't care. I was having the time of my life. I bent to kiss her pale throat, licking a trail to her breasts. I took one nipple into my mouth, then the next, sucking gently at first, then urgently. Her cream had coated my entire hand now as I continued to explore her intimate depths. She begged for more and I began to kiss and slide my tongue down her body — circling her belly button and traveling along the junction of her thigh and groin as I spread her legs wide.

My mouth was watering in anticipation and I could smell her excitement in the air. I needed this, like a drowning man needed land. I longed for her taste. I dipped my head to her slick pussy, flattening my tongue to lave through her folds. I licked slowly up to her swollen clit, circling around, not quite touching, teasing. Over and over, I licked from the bottom to the top, not unlike how I would devour an ice cream cone on a hot summer day, trying to catch every drip and taste every drop.

Oh, the sounds she makes. The words she proclaims. My senses were assaulted in every way. By the sweet taste of her pussy. By hearing the encouragement and exclamations flowing from her lips. By feeling her hands in my hair as she urged me to fuck her with my tongue and mouth. By seeing the folds of her sex glisten as I lapped, again and again. Time stood still and we languished in love and lust.

I didn't think it was possible for this moment to be any greater until she reached down and parted her flushed lips for me, exposing the entrance to her primed passage and the bud of her clit above. It was as if she was saying, "More. I'm all yours." I attached my lips to her swollen button, shaking my head from side to side, slowly then faster and faster, trying to add as many sensations as possible. I didn't want her to cum ... I wanted her to explode. I wanted her to climax on my face and feel her vibrating orgasm against my lips and tongue.

And she did. Gloriously. "Oh god ... oh god ... yes, oh god, yes ..." Her cries poured forth in a melodic display of gratification and satisfaction. Few things on earth make a man feel better than knowing he's ushered his love into nirvana.

I kissed her inner thigh as she came back to me, back to the here and now. I crawled back up alongside her lush body, placing more kisses here, then there, until finally reaching her lips and settling in next to her on the pillows. We held and caressed each other while we cooled down, basking in each other's presence. As the afternoon turned toward twilight, the salt lamp cast a warm, pink glow across our bodies and the edges of the room receded into darkness. Wordlessly, I basked in the simple reality of being her man and of the gratitude I felt for having found each other again, after years apart. When I'm not wrapped up in the energy of her body (the arousal she incites, as she had done again today), I'm consumed by her sweet and incomparable spirit. I had known her for decades — *loved* her for decades — and yet it still surprised me that the noise of my life (work, family drama, chores) disappeared the moment I was with her. She was my definition of "home" even though we'd never shared one.

As if reading my mind, she sighed sweetly. I leaned down and delivered what I hoped was a soul-stirring kiss to her mouth, tracing her lips with my tongue, urging her own tongue into my mouth so I could gently suck it between my lips. I was unable to take my eyes off her face, realizing how much I loved the way her hair fanned out on the pillow. I settled my body between her legs and took a slow, deep breath as she ran her fingers across my chest. I caught her hands in mine and pinned them to the mattress on either side of her, flashing a devilish grin.

I slid slowly into her wet warmth, sighing with an "I love you" as I filled her — hoping to convey all I was feeling with that simple confession. She parted her lips into a sweet smile and the corners of her eyes crinkled almost imperceptibly, but I was watching her every move, appreciating all the subtleties of her precious body and personality, every nuance of the way we made love. In moments like this, when we weren't in a rush, I wanted to make love slowly at first, relishing in the feeling of being consumed, hoping she was enjoying the feeling of my thick shaft stretching her tight. She squeezed me in that delicious way only a woman can, as I bottomed out and began a long, slow withdrawal. "So good, so fucking good," I whispered. "Oh yes, so, so good," she sighed.

I could take no more. As I began to pound my hips into her, she bucked and arched into me. My eyes focused on her beautifully enraptured face. Her eyes, which had been closed as she lost herself in desire, suddenly fluttered open to capture my gaze. The intensity of our lovemaking ramped up to a fever pitch that filled the room with sound — squeaking bed springs, moaning, and the slick sound of our sliding against one another. We proclaimed our love, we urged each other to further heights, until finally as one, the dam burst between us. The rush of my cum poured into her clenching pussy, our juices mingling into the heady scent of spent lovers. Our bodies shook and spasmed through thrust after thrust. Exhausted, satiated, we finally collapsed together in a delirium of love and lust. And as we slowly recovered, the unspoken truth of reaching a simultaneous climax hung between us. This was how love worked. This was how we were meant to be.

She Said ...

I've always thought there was something magical about late summer. The sunsets come too soon but burn brilliantly with orange and pink. The temperature is not too hot and not too cold, and my mood is always tinged with a perfect sort of gratitude for the blossoms and the fresh air, while being blissfully in denial about the long, cold winter ahead. It makes the little things seem that much more important.

I was enjoying that very sense of wonder at the universe that day. It was late afternoon, and I practically skipped from my car to his front door. The front door was unlocked, so I let myself in to find him walking toward the door, drying his hands on a towel.

"Hi!"

He loved it when I acted like I was just stopping by for a cup of tea, even though we both knew I was here for something a little bit hotter. "Neighborly" wasn't really my thing.

His dogs met me at the door, and I crouched down to briefly give them cuddles and kisses before standing upright, crinkling my nose at him, and glancing toward the stairwell.

"After you," he said, and followed me up the steps. I raced up the stairs, flipping off my shoes as I went. At the top, I turned around to see him smiling.

"Kiss m..." I began, but his lips captured mine before I could finish, his hand cupping my jawline firmly but lovingly. I closed my eyes so I could focus on the way he smelled and felt. Like soap. Like love.

He kissed my bottom lip first, soft and full in the middle, coaxing my mouth open to taste my tongue. I was suddenly warm everywhere, needful, and a little weak in the knees. His left hand slid up the back of my shirt, tickling my shoulder blade, trailing lazily back down my spine, stopping with his hand a few inches below my waist band, his palm resting snugly against the upper curve of my ass. He kept kissing me as he dropped his hand from my jaw and moved to unbutton my jeans. I tumbled forward a bit with the release, falling deeper into our kiss.

After all these years, we still undressed each other as if it were the first time — eagerly and curiously and in awe of every inch of skin we uncovered. As we moved into the bedroom, I noticed that the light from outside was shifting toward dusk. I admired the tone of his skin under the soft peach glow of a salt lamp on his bedside table. "Mood lighting …"

"Yep," he said. "I'm romantic like that."

And he was. He pulled back the sheets on the bed, inviting me in. He tucked himself in beside me, like a love letter into a crisp linen envelope. As he kissed and held me gently in his arms, I pressed myself against his warm torso, letting my fingertips flit across a nipple before gripping his chest more tightly. *This. This is where I belong.*

Still kissing me, he held me confidently with his right hand as his left found its way to my thighs, then to the apex of my sex. I opened my legs to welcome him in, shuddering and gasping at that first nerve-awakening moment when his fingers found my folds. I could think of nothing else but the delicious sensation. I reached down to stroke his cock, once, twice, but found myself too overwhelmed by the feeling of his exploring fingers to focus. I settled back and surrendered to his worship. I hoped he didn't mind, and that he knew his moment would come soon enough.

His mouth wandered to my breasts. He licked and sucked and tickled each curve, pulling my nipples into his mouth one by one, all the while never straying in his dedication to pleasuring my pussy. I shifted, pressing my hips harder against his hand. "Yes. More …"

So he slid further down the bed, tossing the sheets and comforter carelessly aside. He spread my legs wide, kissing my belly and then my hip bone as he traveled downward. He grasped my thighs gently but firmly, holding them apart as he lowered his face into my sex, starting at the bottom, licking me in upward strokes.

I closed my eyes and listened to the sound of his tongue as it slipped through the moisture of my arousal. He circled my clit with the tip of his tongue and slid two fingers deep inside me. I cried out in ecstasy. "Oh god! Oh my god! Yes….!" I could literally feel his lips smile against me, satisfied with my response to his efforts.

I clutched the sheets with one hand, trying to ground myself, as my other hand reached down to spread the lips of my labia wide open, giving him more room to play and roam and delight. "Mmmmm…" I heard and felt him say.

I needed release, and, as if he were able to read my mind, he obliged. Like the build-up to a fireworks finale, he shifted from delivering "wow, that's incredible" attentions to "this is so good I might die" stimulation. My trembling grew with his renewed energy. He reached one hand up to hold mine and I was done for. I gripped his hand for dear life and let my body tumble head over heels, wave after wave, muscles quivering through gasped moans, into that beautiful abyss. He never let go. I could feel him kissing my leg, then my ribcage gently, as he pulled himself up to lay his body next to mine.

I rolled over to embrace him, smiling and kissing him as he pulled the blankets back over our bodies. This was perhaps my favorite part of lovemaking — the restful moments of love and gratitude that served as an intermission, allowing our bodies to recover, but that also served the purpose of letting us really see one another in our most vulnerable form. Blissful, tired, but still flushed with passion. Sometimes the pause was just for a few minutes, and sometimes we lay like that for hours, talking and enjoying one another's touch, listening to our hearts beat side by side.

As I recovered from the stupor of my bliss, I couldn't help but feel aroused and playful once again with his skin so close to mine. As I moved to sit up, he stopped me, brushing my tousled hair behind my shoulders and then laying me back down on the pillows. He kissed me deeply as he lifted his body into place between my thighs. In the warm glow of the room, I could see every cord of muscle in his arms, his neck, his chest. I was reminded briefly of a figure drawing class I had taken where the model sat beneath a light in a dim room while we sketched every detail and every shadow. My lover was more beautiful to me than any model, and I didn't want to sketch him — I wanted to worship and be ravished by him.

He clutched both of my hands and pinned them against the mattress, our fingers and intentions intertwined, as he angled his hips forward and slid inside me. Slowly and tentatively at first, pushing bit by bit into me as my body became wetter, more pliable, more desperate to embrace him. And then I was pushing my hips into his, hungry for more. We found our rhythm and locked eyes. He smiled. I said, "I love you." I could feel him so deeply inside me that I imagined I could feel him all the way in my stomach, making me feel full and satisfied in a way that nothing else ever had or would. I flexed my pelvic muscles along his shaft, gripping his cock in a way that made him moan. "It's so good …" he whispered. "So incredibly good," I answered.

The intensity of our combined heat and desire rivaled our very first time together. The rest of the world fell away and there was just this moment. This moment as the sun was setting beyond the bedroom window and here, inside, we reveled in the romance of it all. By the peach-toned light of the salt lamp, our skin looked perfect, ageless, flawless. *It's like a dream.* He was the young man I had fallen in love with all those years ago.

The sheets were draped over his waist, creating a barrier that kept us safely and warmly impervious to the realities of the world. There was only us. My body was building its way toward another orgasm and I instinctively closed my eyes and gripped his hands tighter.

"Oh, god yes …" he muttered, feeling where I was headed.

Don't miss this. Open your eyes. I turned my head to face him and looked deeply into his eyes. In the ethereal glow of the room, their light blue color had darkened and his pupils had blown large with his arousal. I could see into his soul. I could see my love reflecting back at me in their shine.

He was amazing. I have never known anything as surely as I knew this … He was everything. And he was as unapologetically and hopelessly in love with me as I was with him.

His shoulders were square and strong as he balanced above me. My every nerve ending was buzzing with sensation. He leaned in to kiss me. When he pulled back, leaving my lips still parted, he looked at me and smiled that sweet, slow half-smile I loved so much. I took a mental snapshot of him in that moment; I would remember this forever.

There was no holding back anymore ... this was the moment today had been made for. He slid backward, almost entirely out of my body, creating a desperate feeling of emptiness that caused me to raise my hips hungrily, crashing into him just as he thrust deeply back inside. I screamed in pleasure. Again and again, his cock ravenously stroked my pussy, in and out, slowly then quickly, with a sweet smile and a wink, with jaws set ... eyes piercing. I could feel his thighs tensing. I wondered for a millisecond if he could possibly be feeling everything I was feeling in this moment. And then he showed me ... pressing forward as he shot his hot cum into me at the precise moment I bit my bottom lip and shrieked with my own pleasure, jolting and spasming in a simultaneous orgasm, like two people fused by heat and moved by electricity. *I love you, I love you, I love you.*

The moment, the feeling, was so intense that I could do nothing but try to catch my breath and watch our bodies cling to one another, as if I had lost all control and was a mere spectator to our love. He, too, was completely silent ... caught in a whole-body muscle spasm that bent his head backward and stretched his legs, arms, and torso into a delicious curl. Struck with the realization that this kind of mind-blowing sex is a precious gift, a privilege that should never, ever be taken for granted. In that moment, we knew we never would.

Chapter 11
EPIC

He Said ...

At this point, she and I had been in a serious (but on-again, off-again) relationship for nearly a decade. When we were living in the moment, everything was perfect. The love was real, the lust was hot, the respect was mutual. But we tended to go for long periods of time without seeing each other; life would intervene — work stuff, family stuff, personal stuff. Sometimes it would be many months without so much as a kiss, or several weeks without a single word. And that was hard.

When we weren't blissfully living in the *moment* — the whispered professions of love, the unabashed laughter, the soul-affirming sex — it was inevitable that one of us would get too wrapped up in the *past* or the *future*. Between us would then pass so much "but you said ..." and too much "where is this headed?" And we never had good, reassuring, or confident answers for one another. When we got philosophical, things got complicated. This time, complication struck in springtime — the world full of raindrops and possibility — and I was convinced that our love had run its course. I had decided that "complicated" was too complicated.

I wondered, *"What, exactly, was the end-game of our love?"* There had been no promises of marriage vows or picket fences ... not even a predictable schedule or a shared life outside of our private homes or the hotels we frequented. All those years ago, this beautiful journey had started with one simple phrase from her: "I think we should do this." And I was so glad we had. But I felt compelled to book-end that expression now, telling her "I think we should take a break."

I wasn't surprised when she was cool, calm, and collected in the face of "goodbye." We'd both grown in maturity enough to never again get triggered into begging or cajoling or even guilt-tripping. She said, "Wow. Yeah. Okay ... now what?"

I suggested we meet for a beautiful morning together later that week — that we kiss goodbye (and then some), at least for now. And so we did.

It started out perfectly. We were making some amazingly sensual love. My goddess was astride my legs, riding my lengthy shaft slow and steady, eyes meeting as her hips rolled, her hair swaying from side to side, so erotic and beautiful. She slowed her gyrations, slid off, and pivoted deftly on one knee before lowering herself once again onto my slick cock. Oh, my favorite view, her luscious cheeks spread ever so slightly as we became one, affording me the freedom to squeeze and knead, caress and stroke her ass as her wet pussy coated my cock. Only this time, something went awry.

Neither of us realized anything was wrong until after we were cuddled up, basking in after-glow. A slight miscalculation in positioning during that reverse-cowgirl moment, it seemed, had left her injured. Skin torn, bleeding heavily. I wasn't sure what to do as she soaked up the blood — so red against the white towel — but I felt horrible. I had hurt her ... the person I least wanted to hurt in the entire world. As always, she was controlled and reassuring; she insisted she was fine, that I shouldn't feel badly, that "accidents happen."

We eventually made our way back into the bedroom, saying little if anything. I gathered her into my arms in the bed we had left disheveled a few minutes ago. She kissed my chest and breathed softly.

I couldn't relax, so I sat up and sought out my boxers and a t-shirt. And instead of coming back to the bed — to her — once I was clothed, I sat down in an armchair. I'm not sure why I left her on the bed alone, but I felt myself turning inward, ruminating on what had happened and predetermining an early end to our latest adventure. "I'm so sorry," I said.

"It's okay, we'll look back and laugh someday," she said. She gingerly crawled off the bed and walked over to me. She was wearing black panties and nothing else. She was the injured one — surely hurting and even a little scared — but she came over, smiling sweetly, to comfort *me*. *"How does she do that?"* I wondered. She crinkled her nose playfully and smiled, then slowly lowered herself to her knees on the carpeted floor, crouching between my legs.

She laid her hands on my knees and tucked her lower lip between her teeth in an adorable, crooked smile. Her perfectly manicured nails slowly traced a trail up my legs to my inner thighs. My cock gave an appreciative twitch, then another, before hardening again right before our eyes. She nodded and tugged gently on my boxers. I lifted my hips an inch or two above the chair so she could free me from them. I settled back into the chair and spread my knees as her fingertips moved to caress and tickle my balls. She massaged my upper thighs, her thumbs grazing my testes as she moved to wrap both hands around my erection. I laid my head back in ecstasy, closing my eyes in anticipation. The sudden sensation of warmth and the cool trail that followed caused my eyes to snap open. I looked down to catch her beautiful eyes twinkling up at me with mischief as she licked slowly from the base of my dick to its head, lapping at my dribbling pre-cum. She swirled her tongue around the velvety tip, licking up every drop. Lips shining, she stared deep into my eyes and smiled before lowering her lips to my shaft and slowly taking me in.

I was immediately overcome by the whole-body sensation of being engulfed as she pulled my dick deep into her mouth. My breath hitched and my heart began to jackhammer in my chest. I clenched the arm of the chair, holding on for dear life as I fought to control my hips. When her tongue slid over the sensitive underside of my cock, desire exploded in my chest. When her lips surrounded me, tightly, warmly, wetly, I felt it in my knees. As my turgid member was consumed by her, my body was quick to follow.

As the rhythm of her strokes increased, I gently pulled her hair back and held it in one hand, affording me a more thorough view of my dick sliding in and out through her swollen lips — a view I could only maintain fleetingly as the tension built deeply from within. My head was thrown back, every nerve dancing on a knife's edge between uncontrollable ecstasy and complete collapse. I could feel my orgasm building, desperate for release, and before I knew it, my cum was exploding into her mouth as I let out a long moan and a stream of incoherent vocalizations.

I collapsed, satiated, lost in the overwhelming sensation of completion, that feeling of satisfaction as if every task in the world had been finished. Exhaustion based in pure elation washed over me as all my muscles released their tension and my world grew hazy and out of focus along the edges.

The throbbing pulses in my cock slowly ebbed as she lazily, lovingly, drew the last of the hot cum out of me and swallowed it down. As I desperately fought the urge to withdraw my overly sensitive cock, it began to dawn on me … *I'm still hard.* As a rock. This goddess before me could make my body do super-human things. My dick hadn't softened with its release only to swiftly return; it simply had never gone away. Her eyes wide with surprise and delight, she descended once again, slowly, slowly. If she was focused on my pleasure in the first round, the second round provided her a chance to explore and experiment.

The pace of her mouth as it stroked my cock was deliberate and measured. I had the sense of her memorizing every ridge and rise, every vein and texture. One of her hands slid down to gently cup my balls and knead my perineum. Her other hand gripped the base of my shaft. The combination of her warm, wet mouth sliding over me; the massaging of my balls; and the kneading of the sensitive area underneath was driving me crazy. I gathered her hair into my hands once again, gently guiding her strokes as I began to flex my hips into her. The multitude of sensations, and the alluring sight of her head bobbing on my cock finally sent me over the edge … again. Time seemed to slow down as I crested. "Ung … Oh fuck … Oh, baby, yes!" It wasn't wild or frantic, but an overwhelming rush of desire and love. My back arched and my toes curled, one arm gripping the chair as the other still clutched at her hair while I released my seed again. And, once again, I relaxed into exhaustion and utter satisfaction.

"Unbelievable," I sighed.

"You know what's unbelievable?" she asked. "This," she said, waving my still-hard cock at me.

We laughed and smiled at each other. In some magical twist of reality, I needed more. The gleam in her eyes shone in recognition of that fact. There was nothing but primal, carnal desire in our next and final round for that morning. Pure, raw energy of sexual desire filled the room until I couldn't help but plead with her after my third release, "No more!"

I was exhausted, trembling as if electrified. She settled back, her ass upon her heels, looking mighty accomplished and herself a little spent.

Looking back at that day, I am usually left with just one word to describe it: *Wow.*

No man could reasonably expect to have an experience like that, especially in the aftermath of an acrobatic accident. Left to my own devices, I would have kissed her farewell that day, saddened that she had gotten injured and more than a little bummed that our goodbye rendezvous was cut short. It might have been a day I hoped to forget, but turned out to be one of my very favorite memories.

She Said ...

Our relationship is complicated. We love and lust so completely that sometimes it clouds our judgment — sometimes pushes us away from each other as strongly as it pulls us back together. Magnetic, for better or worse.

Across the years, we've said farewell more times than I can count, tearfully and with mutual anguish. Sometimes at his bidding, and sometimes at mine. And, somehow, when the winds are fairer and our hearts a little lighter, we always find our way back to one another. And so it was that we met that morning at a quaint little hotel along the highway to make love "one last time" before taking a break. I had written him a letter, folded and sealed into an envelope, that I planned to give him when we parted that day — a sort of "goodbye for now" love letter. I always knew that farewell, with him, was only temporary, but it still hurt every time. I wanted to leave him with a perfect note so he could remember me as fondly as I needed him to.

We didn't have reservations this time, just hearts full of hope and jumbles of nerves. I was left a little speechless and disappointed when the woman at the front desk told me there were no available rooms at the hotel.

We walked back to the parking lot and I gestured at the hotel next door. Undaunted, I had no problem changing up our plans, as long as we could be together. I opened my mouth to say as much, when he interrupted me, "Let's find a better day. Maybe this wasn't meant to be. We'll reschedule."

I could feel my heart sinking, panic beginning to set in. *No. No, no, no. What if that's just an empty promise? What if he gets back into his car and I never see him again?*

"Please don't go," I pleaded, attempting to keep my voice calm. "I miss you. We've been looking forward to this for so long."

I smiled with as much confidence as I could muster and leaned forward to kiss him softly. "Since when have you known me to so easily take *no* for an answer?"

He shook his head and laughed as he slid into the passenger seat of my car, resting his warm hand on my leg as I put the car into gear.

I could feel my heart rate settling back to something that resembled normal. Beside him, I felt sane. Healthy, happy, complete.

We had luck next door, and moments later, we were kissing and shedding our clothes in a crisp, clean hotel room. The thought that he could have just driven away today was beyond me. And miss *this*? We were perfect together.

Our lovemaking started out slow and sweet. I sat astride him as his head rested against the pillow, my hands gliding over his muscular chest and pert nipples. I rocked my hips, drawing him into me deeply, wetly, listening to him moan softly. I leaned forward, letting my hair tumble onto his shoulders as I kissed him. He lovingly wrapped his hands around my jaw, pulling me deeper into the kiss, causing me to fall forward just a bit, losing my rhythm. I caught myself and planted a kiss on his chest before pivoting my body to leave his handsome face behind me. I ran my hands along his muscular legs and heard him sigh.

Reverse cowgirl. Oh, god, yes. I knew it was what he was thinking, though he didn't say a word. It was a position we both loved, one more lusty than romantic, and hot as hell. Sometimes, it allowed me to watch ourselves in a mirror, which was sort of like viewing our very own private "sex tape" — the idea of which definitely turned me on. But most importantly, it gave him his favorite view, where he could relish the sight of his cock sliding in and out of my pussy behind the generous curves of my ass. He grasped my smooth cheeks, one in each hand, as he controlled my movement on his cock, listening to my moaning grow louder, evolving into primitive phrases like "oh, fuck, it's so deep," and then devolving back to panting and whimpers and cries of ecstasy that caught in the back of my throat.

I was lost in the moment, ravishing and being ravished, when we both picked up the speed and began to slam into one another with reckless abandon. I initially felt no pain, but the next several minutes turned out to be unique. Scary. Quiet. My delicate skin had torn just enough to cause significant bleeding and he was the first to notice all the blood. I told him I was fine and tiptoed to the bathroom to run a towel under warm water and create a hot compress for the injury. He followed me, staying close but clearly not knowing what — if anything — he should do. I was scared when I saw all the blood against the white towel, needing to rinse it down the drain, over and over. I kept breathing in a measured way and thinking: "I am *not* going to the emergency room for vaginal stitches, damn it. This better clot!"

I could already see the humor in it, but remained a little nervous. I could sense that he was more emotional that I was. He tucked my hair behind one ear and kissed my shoulder. I turned to look at him, setting the pink towel on the edge of the sink. "I'm okay," I told him. And I was. I had only the tiniest physical discomfort and the bleeding was slowing down.

I eventually led him back to the bed, where I retrieved my panties and put them back on.

"Every couple deserves a good 'sex injury' story," I assured him. He smiled weakly. We curled up under the blankets in a somber moment of snuggling. I could practically hear the wheels turning in his head — his worry, his unnecessary regret. It's cliché, perhaps, to talk about someone in terms like "he'd never hurt a fly," and yet it was true. And, goodness knows, he'd never willingly hurt *me*. Our love for each other was a sort of extension of our love for life itself. We protected each other and while, yes, we'd hurt each other in the past — through temporary goodbyes or painful misunderstandings — the one thing we had never done is hurt each other on purpose. So I needed to let him know I was okay ... that injuries are simply accidents, and that I was still having fun, and feeling loved.

But I was losing him. He got up, gathering his discarded clothes, and settled into the armchair, clearly upset. I couldn't let him leave like this. I felt a sense of desperation; I didn't want today to end with a story about a mishap, misgivings, or pain. His confidence and happiness were everything to me.

I walked over and kneeled in front of him, kissing his knee, and threading my fingers reassuringly through his. He smiled weakly.

"I'm okay," I said. "I promise. Look at me. Invincible. Sexy, strong, resilient." I said it like I was delivering a motivational speech or narrating a television commercial. I think I even flexed a bicep. He laughed. And so did I.

I raised myself up and kissed his mouth. "Let's try a do-over," I said as I ran my fingernails softly up the insides of his thighs. He sighed. And his body came back to life.

How so many women are resistant to delivering mind-blowing blowjobs is beyond me. They're missing out on the chance to know their partner's body so very intimately, to earn his ultimate trust, to feel the power inherent in creating ecstasy. It's one of my favorite activities — holding the apex of his sexuality in my hands, in my mouth, learning and memorizing every curve and movement, bringing him exquisite pleasure and the delicious emotional collapse that follows. This was going to be epic.

Despite his initially dejected mood, he was quickly overcome with pleasant surprise under my attentive hands. He leaned back in the chair, clutching at the arms, giving himself over to the sensations. I wanted to watch and capture his every expression, but I settled for feeling him and imagining the rest. I swirled my tongue around the head of his cock, listening to him sigh and moan. I closed my eyes, imagining the muscles in his forearms tensing, his toes rigid against the carpeting. I slid him in and out of my mouth, sucking and licking and exploring. He got harder and harder, pulling my hair back so he could see my face more clearly. There was not a selfish bone in this man's body. Even in the midst of being orally pleasured, he was so very much in tune with finding me beautiful and "checking in" with smiles and caresses and eye contact, to ensure I was having as much fun as he. *I was.*

My mouth was filled with his hot, sweet cum as he gave in to a body-rocking orgasm. While he tensed and tremored, pumping his seed into me, his fervor was unflagging, his cock remaining hard between my lips. *Well, color me delighted.* Our adventure had only just begun.

This was going to be fun. Again and again, I changed things up, finding new ways to create sensation, new movements and sounds, eliciting new muscle spasms from his entire body and sexy wordplay from his gorgeous mouth. "I love you," I thought I heard him whisper. I smiled; he couldn't see it, but I'm guessing he felt it, every curve, as I tasted him, rounding out my cheeks, stretching my jaw to its limits.

Two more times. He came twice more, exhibiting a kind of stamina I didn't know was possible. It even scared me at one point when he held his breath and threw his head back in pure euphoria. When I heard him suck breath back into his lungs needfully and moan, I relaxed. *He's okay. He's way more than okay. He hasn't died ... he's simply gone to heaven.*

I shook my head in disbelief and a bit of pride. I felt like a sex goddess and he revered me as one, kissing me and holding me strongly, despite his utter exhaustion at this point. *My god, he's sexy.* I could worship this man all day, every day, and never tire of it. His hard edges, his muscular lengths, his artful curves.

But the day was getting away from us, and reality waited. We dressed slowly, in awe, not wanting to part. When I drove him back to his car, I gave him the letter and said "farewell." He shook his head, telling me he didn't need the letter, all but saying out loud that our morning full of mishaps that ended in such epic pleasure was the universe telling him that our connection was not something to toss aside, even if only briefly and even if life is hard. We were worth fighting for, and always had been.

It was not farewell, after all.

Chapter 12
SENSATION

He Said …

Unfortunately, there are times when life just weighs you down. It captures and holds you in its clutches and threatens to never let go. It's times like these when you have decisions to make. Do you allow yourself to wallow in self-pity or do you find a way to turn things around … even if only for a little while? It's absolutely necessary to find a way to escape from those everyday worries. For those of us who are lucky, that escape can come in the arms of a loved one.

I was struggling with drama at work — a tyrant boss who was unforgiving of his employees, and a nagging sense that I wasn't being paid enough to put up with his shit. I had been working long hours for no extra reward or gratitude, and I was feeling burned out. It's one thing when your job becomes your life *if* your job is also your passion and you absolutely thrive on the energy of your co-workers. That kind of pressure or workaholism can be easy to accept or justify. But for me, my job was *keeping me* from my life. I was unfulfilled and frustrated, but somehow feeling like it was my own fault. And I was tired … bone-weary, physically tired.

I suppose that's why I was starting to second-guess everything in my life right about then. I even began to wonder if throwing myself into my love affair with her was more complicated than necessary. Or if we needed a break. The love was real and the friendship time-tested, but we only saw each other for stolen moments of intimacy. It was all beginning to feel like I wasn't living in the real world — that I was kidding myself or keeping myself purposefully distracted from important decisions I needed to make in my life.

She had invited me over, knowing I was enjoying a rare vacation day, and I had said yes. But my sullen mood traveled with me to her house. I was admittedly pensive, reluctant, and not fully in the moment that day … at least not immediately. But when the door opened just seconds after my knock, and I saw her radiant smile, my armor began to crumble. I stood there a moment, gathering my bearings and gazing upon her gorgeous figure. The ice melted as I leaned into her for the first of what would be many kisses that day. She was always wearing something out of a fashion magazine, even for these brief encounters. Today it was a loose, summery dress, short at the thigh, paired with a denim jacket (which she didn't need inside the house, but that completed the look). She looked stunning as usual, and relaxed and playful to boot.

As if by instinct, my hands made their way to the smooth curves of her ass. I immediately noticed that I could not feel the seam of her panties under the flowing skirt of her dress. I gathered the fabric in my hands and drew the material up and over her hips to reveal only bare flesh underneath. Immediately aroused, I grabbed one of her pale cheeks in one hand as my other moved to find the sweet center between her slightly parted legs. I'm not sure if I had even remembered to say hello; she didn't seem to mind. I felt the soft tufts of hair covering her pussy before slipping a finger into her deliciously warm sex. She moaned softly, spreading her legs further to provide more direct access. With my free hand, I managed to free her from her jacket and slip the dress over her head to leave her naked, a goddess before me.

"Now. Fuck me now," she demanded breathlessly, those three simple words conveying the magnitude of her desire for me. It was an uplifting feeling, to be so needed, so wanted, that this woman, intelligent beyond all belief, would be at a loss for any other words.

I pushed her backward toward the bedroom while she grabbed my belt buckle and began unbuttoning my jeans. I quickly slipped off my shirt as she fell to the bed, her hands on my hips pulling me with her.

She dragged my jeans down over my ass and released my cock, bouncing at full attention and dripping with excitement. Kicking off the rest of my pants, I lifted one of her legs to my shoulder. She let out an audible gasp of anticipation, urging me to impale her in one fluid thrust of my hips. As I drove into her, she arched her back, stiffened her legs, and bit down on her lower lip, writhing in the grip of arousal. Sometimes lovemaking really is just a great fuck, and this was one of those times. We were furious and delirious, frenzied and completely abandoned in the moment. We pounded against one another, hands clutching and squeezing, and mouths sending a torrent of passionate moans into the air.

Collecting myself ever so slightly, I released her leg and lowered my body on top of hers without pulling away from the warmth of her pussy, seeking maximum skin-to-skin contact. I pushed myself up onto the palms of my hands, looked deeply into her eyes, and asked, "Now?" She acknowledged her consent with a quick nod of the head.

Energized, I doubled down on my efforts, driving us higher and higher until both of our bodies crested and fell into breathtaking climaxes. We rolled to our sides on the bed in one another's arms, riding through the delicious aftershocks. The world seemed to fall away and there was nothing but us and our love.

As our breathing returned to normal, she rested her head in the crook of my arm, her dainty fingers tracing patterns on my chest. She looked up with a smile and asked, "Wanna go again?" I huffed a quick laugh, shaking my head in mock exasperation. This lovely woman was insatiable.

She motioned to her bedside table, where a smorgasbord of sex toys had been neatly laid out. Her favorite glass dildo, black ribbons to bind her hands or feet, a girthy, silicone cock I had once watched her ride as it was suction-cupped to the bottom of her bathtub … all present and accounted for. *Hmm, a silk scarf?*

"Pick one," she said, giving me a mischievous smile.

"Blindfold," I responded, an idea taking form in my devious mind.

She reached over me, her rosy nipples grazing my chest, as she grabbed the silky material and drew it back over my skin. I took it from her slightly trembling hand and wrapped it around her head, taking extra care to tie it gently, but firmly. I guided her to lay back, resting her arms at her sides. As she settled in, I maneuvered myself into position, hoping to keep my location a mystery to her. As smoothly and quietly as possible, I leaned over to place a kiss against the inside of her knee. From there, I traced my nose along her inner thigh, causing her to part her legs in invitation. Lifting my head from her body, I leaned forward and breathed a warm sigh next to her glistening sex. The scent of her arousal filled my head enticingly. *"Too soon,"* I thought. More so to divert my path than with any forethought or planning, I slid light fingertips up her opposite thigh, brushing over the fluff of her pubic hair. I surprised her when my tongue traced a quick circle around her belly button before I jumped up to suck one of her stiff nipples deep into my mouth. I ran my nose over her sweet face, licked across her lips, and left her trying to capture my own lips in vain as I moved to breathe heavily against her neck.

I abruptly crawled from the bed, leaving her breathing heavily, clutching the sheets, and wondering where I'd appear next. On light feet, I moved to the other side of the bed, caressing her breasts, touching her belly, brushing her hair from her face. I touched, licked, kneaded, and nibbled in a dizzying, random fashion before positioning myself between her knees. I took my dripping cock in hand and wiped a trail of pre-cum along her thigh, teasing her into believing I was giving in to my own excitement. Instead, I firmly pushed her knees out and back as I slid to my belly. I pounced on her sex, my tongue diving into her wet folds. I used my hands to open her flushed lips wide, holding them aside to provide complete access to her waiting pussy. I plumbed her depths with my tongue, replacing it with first one, then two fingers. As I pistoned my fingers in and out, feeling her cream coat my hand, I assaulted her clit with my tongue. I sucked her lips into my mouth and lapped up her essence. The wails, moans, and expletive-laced cries she unleashed were beautiful. I could feel her vaginal walls clenching at my fingers, her hips pushing against my tongue, all in an effort to drive herself to climax. "Good girl, let it go, cum for me."

I sat back on my heels, enjoying the sights and sounds of her orgasm. I smiled in happiness, content in the knowledge that no matter what life threw at me, she could always find a way to gather me in, to be in the now, to be hers. And I was.

She Said ...

It's been a long time since I could pass for a teenager or be someone's "summer fling," but I still liked to dress for him the way he saw me: young, playful, carefree, girly, an intoxicating mix of innocent girl-next-door and sex-hungry vixen. And so it was that I was wearing a pink and white sundress that day, with a denim jacket thrown over it. And no panties.

He was quiet from hello, pensive and distracted. But he was still clearly aroused and game for whatever I had in mind. I slowed down my instinct to skip my way to the bedroom. I knew he needed a moment. So I just stood there, looking into his eyes, smiling softly to let him know that it was okay. That we were okay. That whatever he was feeling or going through, it would be okay. Time stood still as he kissed me deeply. The curves of his lips, the way he held my waist then touched my cheek ... it was all perfect. But something was off. There was a sadness, a distance I couldn't breach.

I knew he was struggling at work and I suspected his mood might have been caused by a frustrating phone call from his boss or by any number of stressors in his life. I felt sad as I noticed that he wasn't quite himself, but then I got lost in that first kiss.

Maybe I should have stopped and asked him if he needed to talk, but I was warm and wet and in a come-fuck-me kind of mood. I shivered and giggled when he slid his hand up my thigh, lifting the edge of my dress and discovering that I was naked underneath. "Oh, my," he said. He gave one cheek a little squeeze then trailed a finger through my pubic hair, parting my skin just enough to feel my juices. Just enough to make me moan and glance down the hallway toward my bedroom.

He took my hand and obliged, kicking his shoes off as we traveled. In one swift motion, he pulled my dress over my head and dropped it in our wake. I was completely nude, and grappling with his shirt, his belt, his zipper. I fumbled and grumbled the way someone might if she were starving to death and found the pantry secured with a padlock. I wanted him and I wanted him now. He helped me strip him down to nothing but a watch. I fell back onto the bed and literally pulled him on top of me.

"Now. Fuck me now."

He raised his eyebrows but didn't argue. He spread my legs wide, lifting one up over his shoulder to provide better access, and gave me one last view of his huge, throbbing cock, glistening with pre-cum at the tip, before driving his shaft deep inside me. It was exactly what I needed. Hard and fast and hot and wordless. The kind of "I-need-you-now" sexual experience that we rarely got to entertain, but both seemed to be craving in that moment. It was delicious. We were rocking so frantically in that moment that I couldn't tell if the noise I was hearing in my ears was the bed creaking or my heart racing. With every thrust, I could feel the nerve endings in my pussy becoming more and more sensitive. "Oh, god," I kept gasping, running out of breath, my mouth dry and my body so full of pleasure.

"Now?" he asked and I nodded.

It was exactly what I needed — complete, utter abandon, fists clenching, backs arching, penetration that was deep and full, hard and fast. I have no idea if it lasted five minutes or fifteen, but it was a delicious "quickie" that left both of us breathless. He collapsed on top of me, and I giggled. "Hi," he said to underscore the fact that we had just gone from hello to orgasmic delight without pretense, foreplay, or niceties. "Hi," I crinkled my nose, which he promptly kissed, then pulled the sheets over my shoulders and held me gently in his arms.

I closed my eyes and rested my head on his shoulder. I heard him sigh, and it sounded sweet and satisfied but still a little sad and distracted. I knew something was wrong, but I wasn't sure whether it was about me, or whether pointing it out made things better or worse. I really just wanted to help him shake whatever had a gloomy hold on his heart or his mind that day. But did moving from sex to afterglow to more intimacy make me selfish, when clearly something was wrong?

I can't deny that I was more than a little worried that he might be withholding difficult news from me — that perhaps he was going to relocate (something he talked about often, but that I was in denial of because I couldn't imagine him leaving me). Or maybe he was upset with me about something I'd said or done recently? (I tended to put my foot in my mouth when it came to him, and I'm not sure why.) Without thinking, I opened my mouth to ask, "Is everything okay?" But I stopped myself. I suspected that if he wanted to talk about it, he'd start that conversation. So I said nothing. I chose to embrace the silence.

In all our years together, the silence is one of the things we've mastered in a way that many other couples have not. He's the only man I've ever been able to be in silence with — for minutes or hours — and feel totally safe, comfortable, unjudged, and completely loved. There's a song about that feeling, I think. Something about, "You say it best when you say nothing at all."[1]

Eventually, he sat up and rested his back on the headboard of the bed. I pulled myself up to sit next to him. "So ..." I broke the silence. "Wanna do that again?" I asked devilishly. He smiled and shook his head in a not-yes-not-no sort of wobble, while rolling his eyes just a tiny bit. In my head, I could hear him saying, *"This woman is insatiable. I love that about her, but she's going to exhaust me!"*

I gestured to the collection of sex toys on the bedside table. "Pick something," I urged. "We'll play a game!"

"Blindfold," he said, giving me his crooked smile. I picked up the length of colorful silk from the table and dragged it softly over his skin.

He pulled it from my hands and wrapped the silk around my head, tying it firmly over my eyes, leaving the tails of the fabric to trail through my hair and tickle my shoulders.

I can't remember if he said the words, "No talking" or if I just knew that was the first rule of engagement. I laid down on my back and waited, keeping my hands relaxed at my sides. *What was he doing?*

---

1   "When You Say Nothing at All," written by Paul Overstreet and Don Schlitz, 1988.

Then I felt it ... a kiss on the inside of my knee, which gave me goosebumps. I bit my bottom lip and waited for the next sensation.

His nose on my inner thigh.

Cool air where my leg joined my pelvis.

The tip of a tongue just above my belly button.

A nibble of his perfect teeth on my right nipple.

A kiss on my upper arm.

Hot breath on my neck.

Something slippery and warm and wet sliding up my thigh.

Then nothing. My breath caught in anticipation. It was so quiet in the room that all I could hear was the air conditioning whooshing through the vents of the house. My only indication that he was still there was from a periodic shifting of the bed as he moved about.

In the silence behind my blindfold, I kept thinking back on his state of mind, wondering if he was really enjoying this or just humoring me. *Shut it off*, I thought. *Be in this moment.*

I felt my breathing slow and a sense of calmness spread through my chest like warm honey. I was so relaxed. I trusted him so completely and felt so safe with him that I forgot to anticipate his next touch. "Oh!" I exclaimed when, in one swift movement, he changed the game entirely. I felt pressure on the insides of my knees as he spread my legs like a butterfly's wings, and then he was consuming my pussy, leading with his tongue, following with his lips, teeth, nose.

I was salivating in every way ... my mouth, my body, my heart. He drew circles around my clit, then pressed his fingers inside me, searching, teasing, exploring. I bucked my hips into him, hoping that returning a bit of his pressure and heat wasn't against the unspoken rules of this new game. I heard him whisper, "Yes. Good girl. Go slow ..."

But going slow wasn't the theme of the day. I clutched the sheets in my fists and moaned. I opened my eyes behind the blindfold, stealing glimpses through the folds of silk — of his shoulders between my thighs, of his succulent ass raised near the end of the bed, out of reach.

I wanted to touch him so badly, but I trusted him to lead me, as I crested through a delicious wave of passion. He flicked my clit with his fingertips, licked me hungrily, spread me wider. I was done for. Spasm after spasm of orgasmic delight, I unleashed my ecstasy into the silent room. "Yes, baby, yes," I heard him murmur into my body. "Let it go ..."

And I knew. I knew I'd always feel him when I closed my eyes, hear him in the silence, and trust that he'd come to me, even when I couldn't quite reach him. I knew.

And I still do.

Until Next Time:
A NOTE TO OUR READERS

As we close the pages of this — our very first — book, we find ourselves humming the 1983 song "Faithfully" by Journey, and the musical interlude is more than just happenstance. A song about lovers who are frequently apart but faithfully in love, it reminds us that every moment — even a brief or stolen moment — spent with someone special is a gift. It prompts us not to focus on the solitude or the sadness of separation, but to celebrate the reunions. The lyrics, as penned by Journey keyboardist Jonathan Cain, say it best:

> "[B]eing apart ain't easy on this love affair.
> Two strangers learn to fall in love again.
> I get the joy of rediscovering you …
> I'm forever yours, faithfully."

That, beloved readers, is what we were hoping to share with you in this most intimate book — the joy of discovering yourself and your lover(s) and then discovering yourselves all over again. In the lives of our *He Said, She Said* characters, there was much to learn and relearn. But two things remained reliably true — love never fails, and farewell doesn't always mean goodbye.

You too, can have beautiful, hot, steamy, inventive romances. It starts with trust and respect, and we happen to think that love matters too. Have faith. And courage. And creativity. Let your walls down enough to love and be loved, to lust and be lusted after. Know that your body is beautiful and your fantasies can be magical, that it's okay to giggle during sex, that "dirty talk" is likely to make their day, and that there is nothing more human and natural and pure than desire.

It is our sincere wish that the stories in this book remind you that, while our individual and gendered approaches to sex and romance are varied (i.e., that what "he says" and what "she says" sometimes tell different stories from radically different vantage points), it is that cross-section of experience — the shared emotions and sensations and pleasure — that bring us together, again and again. Never settle for less than having a real voice in the bedroom (or the hotel room or the elevator or the living room or the hot tub …); never do less than meeting each other halfway, of finding just as much pleasure meeting your partner's needs as you do in receiving fulfillment of your own. Go be adventurous. Go discover. Go love.

Brace Yourself...

THE SECOND GIBBS & BLACK BOOK IS RELEASING SOON!

If you loved *He Said, She Said* — as a solo reading adventure or as an inspirational how-to for yourself and your partner — you'll love what's coming next. Get ready for *Stolen Moments*, a collection of stories about mind-blowing quickies and unlikely hook-ups.

Follow the authors at www.GibbsAndBlack.com to be among the first to know when the new book hits bookstores.

Gibbs & Black are on social media!

@GibbsAndBlack on Instagram, Facebook, Twitter and more!

Made in the USA
Middletown, DE
30 September 2021